MW01133821

MELANIN

DANYELLE BUTLER

MELANIN

iUniverse books may be ordered through booksellers or by contacting:

iUniverse
1663 Liberty Drive
Bloomington, IN 47403
www.iuniverse.com
844-349-9409

ISBN: 978-1-6632-0518-6 (sc)
ISBN: 978-1-6632-0519-3 (e)

Library of Congress Control Number: 2020912888

Print information available on the last page.

iUniverse rev. date: 08/13/2020

PROLOGUE

I watched his chest heave up and down with every single breath. The silhouette of his wife was clinging to his side as she snuggled under his chin. The moonlight poured through the windows and landed onto his eyes. His sandy brown eyelashes curled to perfection as I clenched my jaw. I was in the process of studying him. I wanted to figure out what his possible reactions would be if I gave him a rude awakening. My pistol was resting in my right hand as I tilted my head to the left. I brushed the tip of the pistol against the side of his face awaiting for him to awaken. His eyelids fluttered before it allowed his eyeballs sight. I placed the pistol to my lips and let out a silent hush. Fear danced around his irises as anxiousness filled me. I was in control. I would like it to stay that way. I motioned my head towards the door and he shook his head slowly.

I stood back as he removed his wife's arm from around his torso. He swiftly grabbed for his pajama pants and put it on. I began to grow impatient. I grabbed his hair and pulled him towards the door. We both made our exit out of the bedroom and I instructed him to take a seat on the couch.

"Who are you?" He whispered.

I licked my lips and smirked.

"Carl Koenig. You've been working for the Jackson Mississippi Police Department for five years. Your mother and father are both deceased but they did work in the justice system so that just proves that the apple doesn't fall far from the tree. You've been married to your wife for eleven years and created two beautiful children that attend Jackson Elementary School. You look young for a forty-five-year-old man. Humph. You see, I know a lot about you but I just can't see why you make the stupid decisions you make. You're supposed to be an officer that serves and protects us citizens from harm *not* to be the root of the problem that can potentially get someone killed. Someone innocent. You took something from me that I will never get back. You probably don't even have a clue about what that could be."

Sweat began to form on the side of his face as his breathing increased. He edged towards the end of the couch and rested his arms on his knees.

"Just tell me what you want from me. Go ahead, name your price." He spoke.

"Unfortunately, what I want from you doesn't require your money. But, what I do want, is justice."

I began to approach him slowly as he sat back on the couch with his hands continuing to rest on his knees. I'm trying to read him but I just can't. Something doesn't feel right. He kicked the coffee table over and it crashed into me. I fell to the floor as Koenig ripped something from the table. He wielded a gun that was secretly hiding underneath. My breathing increased.

"Leave the gun on the floor and stand up slowly." He demanded with his gun drawn.

I stood up slowly with my hands up.

"Walk towards me. Try anything, and you're dead." He threatened.

Every step I took my fear grew stronger and stronger. I heard someone open a door and a voice followed behind it.

"Honey?" Koenig's wife called out.

Due to the darkness of the room, I could still only make out the silhouette of his wife standing by the wall, tilting her head in confusion. I quickly shifted my attention back onto Koenig to witness him looking at his wife. I should take advantage of his unawareness. I kicked his leg as he got down on one knee in pain. His gun was pointed at me as he was about to pull the trigger. I swiftly hit his arm as a bullet whizzes past my ear. Loud ringing filled my ears as I covered them in pain. As I was looking down, I saw his gun on the floor. I was about to remove my hands from my ears until Koenig punched me in the face which sent my body flying to the floor. I crawled towards the gun but before I could make it there, he flipped me over. His large hands wrapped around my neck and constricted. It was slowly getting harder to breathe. I clawed at his face as he jerked his head back to continue to choke me. I dug my thumbs into his eyes until he let me go. He held his eyes while screaming. I stood up, grabbed the gun and pointed it in between his eyes.

I looked to where Koenig's wife was standing to view her shirt littered with blood. She sat against the wall while taking short cut off breaths. Everything grew silent around me as shock stunned my body. I tried to swallow the lump in my throat and tried to blink back the tears. Before I could look back to where Koenig was sitting, I heard a gunshot go off.

ONE

INFLUENCE WHAT'S RIGHT

My palms began to sweat as I rubbed my hands together in deep thought. I glanced over at my team as they were adjusting their papers on the desk. I took deep breaths to clear my mind for whatever topic Mr. Davis has prepared for us. I know this isn't the real game but I don't want to be shown up by anybody. Mr. Davis cleared his throat while fixing his tie.

"Is everybody ready?" Everyone shook their heads. "Alright. Is the death penalty appropriate or should it be banned? Team One, what's your statement?"

My team faced me and nervousness crept up my spine. I stood up from my chair and placed my attention on Mr. Davis.

"The death penalty is certainly a cruel, unruly punishment. You see, the perpetrator may have done some unreasonable things but that doesn't mean sentence him or her to death. I believe that once people realize the wrong they have done, they can change. I'm not saying release them once they develop some common sense but at least let them take some accountability for their actions. They can't do that if they're quickly put to death." I reasoned.

"So, you want it to be banned?" Mr. Davis challenged.

"Of course. It just seems barbaric."

Mr. Davis nodded his head in approval and faced the other team. I sat down as my teammates gave me a thumbs up and patted me on the back.

"Alright, anything to follow that up, Team Two?" Mr. Davis asked.

I looked over and saw Connor stand up. He looked over to me.

"I disagree. Let's put this into perspective, shall we? Let's say, a guy takes a car and rams it into thirteen people. He gets convicted. You want this man to live freely in jail without bail so he can rethink his actions? No. It's not barbaric to show justice. It's common sense."

I clenched my jaw in frustration. I quickly stood up from my chair, which surprised Mr. Davis.

"Common sense to put someone to death? Come on, now. Let's stay on your little *scenario.* You never know what someone can go through to be placed in that type of situation. He could be mentally unstable and wasn't taking his medication or he was just outraged by something that was going on in his life. If that case may be, I believe everyone deserves a second chance to at least get some type of peace in their mind."

"Ms. Morris—"

"That may be true but those types of people don't deserve second chances. We are talking about a person who just doesn't give a damn. They could snap your neck and laugh about it and you want them to have peace? No, Jade. It's just not right." Connor interrupted.

"*Those types of people?* What kind of people? Black people—"

"Oh, please. Don't make this a race thing."

"No, I will. See, it's people like you that categorizes others by their records. Someone could have a criminal record for stealing way back in the day and still get hell about it in their current time. The system is screwed. Once you get in a little trouble with the police you're automatically known as a *thug*. That right there alone is why some of us African Americans can barely get jobs because of the messed up system."

"Yeah, that's why..." Connor breathed as he rolled his eyes.

I clenched my jaw.

"Alright, enough from you two. Jade you were supposed to let one of your teammates respond. As well as you, Connor. You both may be the team leaders but you have to follow the rules. You say something, your teammates pick it up, and you have to depend on them for backing you up and saying a credible statement. That's what being a team is about. We have one week until Finals. I expect you to come up with better arguments and better sportsmanship. You got me?" Everyone nodded once again. "You're all dismissed."

I packed up my things and slung my bag over my shoulder. I was about to leave until Mr. Davis called me and Connor to approach him. We did as we were told.

"I know you both are very passionate about one another but you have to sometimes put those emotions you have under a rug until Finals are over. You're letting your emotions cloud your judgment. Just imagine how you or Connor will react if one of you says the wrong thing." I looked down at my shoes. "Exactly. This passive aggressiveness needs to stop. I'll be in my office if you two ever need to talk to me. Understood?"

"Yes, sir." I answered.

"Yes, Mr. Davis." Connor replied.

"Alright. I'll see you both tomorrow."

We both walked towards the hallway in an awkward silence. I glared at him and gripped my bag strap.

"You didn't have to embarrass me like that, Connor." I spoke finally.

"Embarrass you? Jade, there are going to be much tougher people at Finals. I'm trying to prepare you to reach your full potential. I may get a little overboard but just know I mean well." He stopped walking to face me. "I'm sorry."

His light green eyes gleamed with guilt. I smiled while leaning my head to the right. I placed my hand onto his cheek.

"You're forgiven. Thanks for being honest with me." I looked at my hand that was on his cheek while my watch that laid comfortably on my arm caught my eye. I quickly read the time. "Oh, shit. I gotta' go. I'll call you?"

"Certainly."

I pecked his lips before I ran out of the school. I stopped at the nearest bus stop and waited for the bus to come through. I sat down on the bench and whipped out my phone.

4

Mount High is one helluva school. It is the best high school we have here in Jackson, Mississippi. Most high schools are very run down and the education system is terrible. The system here gets worse each time you graduate a grade. So, just imagine what we are going to be *taught* in college. On top of all of this, Mount High is a predominantly white school. I stick out like a sore thumb. If I hadn't joined the Debate Team, I would've been a loner for the past four years.

I quickly texted my mom to let her know I'll be running a little late. As soon as the bus pulled up, I boarded. I took my seat and glanced out of the window. It's funny that once you get deeper in the city, everything changes. Poorly owned government properties along with people living paycheck to paycheck and an area where drug afflicted people roam the streets like zombies is what I like to call my home.

I'm a seventeen year old African American girl whose future is already made up for in today's society. In their eyes, I'm supposed to be under the care of a guy who is affiliated with gang activity while I'm sitting at home with a cigarette hanging loosely in between my lips with no insight on my future. Yeah, I'll pass. I'll most likely see myself sitting in an expensive desk writing my sixth best selling poem. That's more like it.

Mount High is so different from my elementary school. Just reminiscing about the old days really crack me up. I remember when the teachers couldn't control the students at all at my school. They were either on their phones, balling up papers and shooting them across the room like basketball, or trying to get someone's number. As for me, my head was in the books. Grasping as much needed information I could get from that corresponding chapter. The students would tease me about that, especially my best friends Regina and Michael. It got so bad that they had to start carrying around dictionaries to hold a conversation with me. It makes me laugh every time I think about it. Now, that's the only thing I can think about.

Of course, my best friends weren't able to come to the same high school as me which was a factor of our friendship straining apart. Me and Michael sometimes communicated back and forth until we stopped. Not intentionally, though. Something was just taken from him and that something really motivated me to do what I do now. Influence what's right.

I tugged on the bus cord and stood up from my seat. I wobbled to the doors until they opened once the bus made a complete stop. I got off, walked across the street, and entered into my mother's diner.

"You have tables to clean so get to it." My mother announced as soon as I picked up my apron. "Chop, chop. Time is money and you're already drilling into my paycheck by being late."

"I texted you to let you know—"
She held her hand up.

"Tables."
I sighed.

I picked up a rag on my way to the stained tables. I began to wipe up the mysterious stains which made my stomach turn. As I was wiping, I overheard my mother talking to one of the cooks about a website that I know all too well.

"Did you see the headline on that Melanin website?" My mother asked.

"Did I? He or she exposed the hell out of that police officer last night. I mean, it was so brutal. They had the video footage as well as the description the cop was trying to sell to a minor. A black one at that." The cook responded.

"Yeah, that's crazy. Just imagine how many other dirty cops are probably doing the same or worse." My mom paused. "Do you think it's too brutal? Don't get me wrong, the idea of the website is amazing but to a certain extent. These are people's lives he or she is messing with. Just imagine what those people will do if they strike back."

My heart dropped.

"The person is anonymous. I'm pretty sure that the creator of the website is smart enough to not leave any digital footprints that'll get him or her exposed. I'm not saying that they can't slip up but if they do, I'm pretty sure they will have that handled." I interjected while stopping my cleaning. They both looked at me. "Just a thought."

I continued my work. Their words soon began to slither in and out of my ears as I played a scenario in my mind. What if someone comes for that person? Will *they* be ready?

TWO

KEEP YOUR COMPOSURE

I wipe my hand across the foggy mirror to see my round face and dark brown eyes. Water traveled down the side of my dark mocha skin and made its destination to the end of my chin. I swiftly licked my lips as dimples pierced my cheeks. I sighed at the sight of my face. I never thought I was a pretty girl. I wasn't lucky enough to have the influence of my dad to raise my self-esteem and to help me acknowledge my self-worth. You would think my mom would be capable of filling my dad's shoes but her main focus is raising me and getting me the hell out of the house. I sighed as I rolled my eyes.

I picked up my comb and tugged at the ends of my hair. It took me a couple of tries to finally get my hair untangled but once I did, I raked the comb through the longer parts of my hair. My hair only reaches to the top part of my shoulders. That only adds onto the list of my insecurities. Especially, when you're in school with Caucasian girls with hair down their backs. I placed the comb down and picked up the brush. I brushed my hair up into a ponytail and grabbed the thin headband and slung it around my head. I made a face in the mirror.

"Good enough." I breathed.

I tightened the towel around my chest and walked out of the bathroom. As I stepped out, I accidentally bumped into my mom.

"Damn, are you going to knock me over?" My mother commented, rudely. "Anyway, I need you to work a double tonight."

"Double? When will I have time to do my homework?"

"Whenever you get off of work. Don't act brand new. You know Wednesdays are hectic. Now, I need you there. If not, it's your ass."

She walked away from me as I rolled my eyes. A trail of her scent embraced me. I always loved the way my mother smelled. She had that scent that made me want to hug her and never let go. It just reminds me of when times were much better. When I was younger and didn't know anything. When I felt protected because I was vulnerable. Now, it's just a cold shoulder. Since I'm in high school, she expects me to be a grown woman who can take care of herself but I'm far from that. Just because I come of age that doesn't mean I don't need love anymore. That's the time when I need more love than ever.

I entered inside of my bedroom and put on my bra and underwear. I stood in front of the mirror and viewed my thin body. I have a body of a twelve year old.

I'm really surprised Connor found an interest in me. There are plenty of other girls at that school who look ten times better than myself. I finished getting dressed and grabbed my bag to exit out of the house. I'm so not in the mood to digest breakfast right now. This is such a depressing morning.

I found the nearest bus stop and sat down on the bench. I looked around and began to take the atmosphere in. I try to leave my problems at home so once I enter into the real world, it'll look like I have everything together. I don't want to be moping around because nobody would want to be around a depressed sack of shit all day. Hell, I don't even want to be around that. Ain't that hypocritical?

"Very…" I agreed out loud.

Someone walked past and nervousness erupted in my stomach. I hope she didn't hear me say that. I also hope she doesn't think I talk to myself. I mean, everyone thinks out loud sometimes. The girl and I locked eyes as I immediately recognized this person. I was hoping I was never going to run into her again. She stopped walking and turned around to face me. Her hazel eyes dilated as the memories we had suppressed against her mind. Wind blew through her light brown hair and clung to her lips that were lathered in lip gloss.

"Jade?"

I placed a fake smile onto my face.

"Yeah. Hey, Regina." I responded.

"Oh, wow. You look good. Long time no see."

"Yeah." Was the only thing I could get out of my mouth. It was so awkward I wanted to shrivel up and hide in my shoes. "How's everything going?"

"It's going well, I can't complain." Regina answered as I noticed something was off about her. "You still go to that white school?"

"Mount High? Yeah."

"Oh, girl! You are probably gon' get into that rich college and get a bomb ass job. Don't forget about me if you start making millions."
I chuckled lightly.

"It's good talking to you again. I know our friendship ended badly and I apologize for that." She paused. "It seemed like you went ghost after the funeral. I haven't seen you around at The Spot since he passed."

The Spot. I haven't heard about that place in a long time. After school, Regina, Michael and I - along with a few other students - would go down to the alleyways until we found the white trailer with graffiti all on it, by the railroad tracks.

At the time, we would treat people wrong, party all night, and sometimes get high on what they were selling. Although we didn't sell dope, the atmosphere really had an affect on us. We were so young and dumb they would call us their *little troopers*. We eventually grew out of the rebel state once we graduated eighth grade. Well, I can't say all of us. Regina would sometimes go down there and sell a couple of things just to provide for her low income family. I couldn't blame her. I probably would do the same thing if I was in her shoes. Michael on the other hand, he completely avoided it. His brother was shot and killed over there because he wanted to be in a gang. His brother felt like he didn't have a family back at home. Well, at least that's what I heard. He's been in a gang for so long he felt like that was his family.

He felt like it was his home. Until his so-called *family* betrayed him.

Just thinking about that place really makes my skin crawl. After being with certain people and building a foundation with them, they will be so quick to tear it down and build something new. Something better. They would do it no matter the cost. No matter who is in their way. As long as they get what they want, they're satisfied.

"Yeah. You know that really wasn't my scene anyway." I answered after a while.

"Well, it was nice seeing you, Jade. I'm sure Michael would be really proud of you." She took out a piece of paper and a pen from her purse and wrote down numbers. She handed the finished product to me. "Call me. I want to try and rekindle our friendship especially because of the circumstances."
I nodded.

She walked away and I watched her go. A little piece of me really missed my best friend. The good and the bad times were spiraling back leaving me on an emotional rollercoaster. I took a deep breath. There's too many emotions going on this morning. The bus crept up and its screeching tires came to a stop. I quickly boarded, took a seat and stared out the window.

I softly knocked on the open door and viewed Michael's back. He turned his head, looked at me, and turned back around to stare out the barred window. I slowly approached him and sat next to him on the bed.

"Are you okay?" I asked with a lot of sorrow in my voice.

His red eyes gleamed at me.

"What the hell do you think, Jade?"

"Look, I can't even lie to you and say I know what you're feeling. But, I will tell the truth and let you know I am here for you every step of the way. You're my best friend and I will always have your back. I know you and your brother were close and I'm really sorry about what happened to him. If you will allow me, I want to be here for you."

Michael's jaw tightened as he clutched his hand together. He began to rock back and forth and I can tell he's about to have an emotional breakdown. I quickly got up from the bed, kneeled in front of him, and pulled him downward into a hug. His tears damped the side of my shirt as he squeezed me tightly. His vulnerability allowed me to pull away and wipe the tears from his face. Michael took a long glance at me and placed his hand onto my chin. His soft plump lips landed onto mine and stayed there for which seemed like forever. Guilt seeped into my heart which caused me to pull away.

"Don't lie to me, Michael. You already know how I feel about you. You can't play with my emotions like this." I explained while holding back my tears.

"I'm not lying to you, Jade. I like you. I've always had—"

"You haven't!" I shouted. My voice started to crack as tears began to stream down my face. "Nobody does. My mom doesn't love me. I'm just her employee without pay. My dad left. He doesn't love me. Society tells me that they do but I know in my heart that they don't. So, don't lie to me, Michael. I'm already sorting through enough lies."

Michael chewed on his bottom lip in deep thought.

"Jade, I—"

"No. Don't *ever* let those words fall out of your mouth again until you mean it." I interrupted.

I sniffed, stood up, and stormed out of the room.

I felt someone tap my shoulder and I shot up from my sleep. The bus driver pointed outside as I turned my head to look at my school.

"You get on this bus a lot. It'll be a shame if I just let you stay asleep as I drive through the city."

"Oh my god, thank you. I didn't even notice when I fell asleep."

"You're welcome. Don't let it happen again. I won't be too generous next time."

I nodded my head and got off of the bus. I walked into the school and immediately looked around for Connor. Besides the Debate Team, I absolutely have no friends. Connor is my boyfriend, of course, but he's also a really good friend to me. I count on him when I'm in need and he comes through when I need him too.

In a failed attempt to find Connor, I walked straight to my locker and something written on it caught my eye. I read the disturbing remarks. *Slut. Whore. Bitch.* I looked around and everyone was staring at me while laughing. The words were written all over my locker in huge letters so everyone can see. A girl with dirty blond hair and blue eyes pushed through the crowd. Mascara weighed heavily on her eyelashes making the appearance of them look like spider legs. Her lips were over lined with lipstick as she smiled mischievously showing her bright white teeth.

"Ladies and Gentlemen, that's what happens when you mess with someone else's man." She announced while laughing. "Side chick."

Everyone began to chant *side chick* while clapping. I grabbed my bag and pushed through the crowd to make it towards the bathroom. Once I made it, I locked myself in a stall. A string of humiliation washed across my face as anger arose in my chest. What are they talking about? I know Connor hasn't been the most faithful person in the beginning of our relationship but I always forgave him and gave him chances to improve himself. He promised he wasn't going to do this to me again.

Nobody has taught me how a man is supposed to treat me. I just know that I am lonely and if a guy shows me just a little bit of attention, I'm hooked. I know it's wrong but, I can't help it. But, the thought of Connor stepping out on me in this stage of our relationship, hurts me. Keep your composure, Jade. They just want to see you break and that's not a show I'm willing to give.

THREE

REMINISCE

The mirror reflected a broken girl. Tears stained my cheeks as every emotion stung in my heart. I gripped the sink. Their harsh words kept replaying in my head over and over again as I began to hyperventilate. Tears rushed down my face as I tried to catch my breath. I can't believe I'm letting them get to me. I try to be strong and be there for myself but sometimes I need support by someone else. Someone who I can always run to in a time of crisis and just know that they'll always have my back. I reached into my pocket and retrieved the piece of paper that Regina gave me. My eyes roamed the paper as I slowly drifted into deep thought.

Should I call her?

I shook the loose thoughts out of my head and tried to cheer myself up. I can't go into class looking like a wreck.

I turned on the faucet and let the cool water caress my hands. I lowered my head and landed my face into the welcoming water. The water seemed to seep into my pores and refreshed me. I rose up and looked back into the mirror and took a deep breath.

"You got this, Jade. Don't worry about what other people say. They're just words." I finally spoke.

I grabbed my bag that was resting on the side of the stall and slung it over my shoulder. I pushed the bathroom door open and looked both ways. Empty. The bell must've rung and I was too busy moping to hear it. I quickly walked to class.

I took a deep breath before I entered the classroom. The room instantly filled with laughter and judgement. The teacher instructed everyone to settle down before she placed her full attention on me.

"Do you have a note?" Ms. Collins asked me.

I shook my head, no.

Ms. Collins took a long look at me until she brushed it off and told me to take a seat. I gripped my bag strap and made my way through the aisles of desks. I felt someone's leg under mine and before I could intentionally react, I tripped and landed on the side of an empty desk next to me. Laughter bounced off the walls and embarrassment whipped me across the face. I finally took my seat and shoved my face into my arms on the desk.

"Alright, class. As you all know, we've been discussing the different techniques about writing and how to form your ideas onto a piece of paper, correctly.

Now, I'm going to put you all in for a little test." Everyone groaned. "Trust me, this shouldn't be difficult unless you weren't paying attention. I want you all to create a poem about how you feel about today's society. This can range from anything that is currently going on or something that might have taken place two years ago. I really want everyone to tap into their feelings and really discuss what you decide to write about is good or bad. Now, this particular assignment is going to be due next Monday. Considering that today is Friday, you'll have plenty of time to complete this over the weekend."

I removed my head from in between my arms to see Ms. Collins grabbing a stack of papers from off of her desk. She began to walk down the aisles.

"I'm passing out the rubrics for what is required in order to get a passing grade. This should be an interesting assignment for me to really get to know you all as individuals and tap into what you're thinking about." Ms. Collins approached me and looked down at me. "This should be a piece of cake for you, Jade. All your writing assignments are incredibly put together. I can't wait to see what you're going to turn in Monday morning."

She met my gaze and I immediately looked away. The paper landed on my desk and I swiftly took a look at it before putting it in my bag. Ms. Collins began her lecture as I slowly drifted into my own world.

I traced my finger across the different bumps and uneven wood patterns in the desk as I shifted in my seat. Music from that night filled my ears and I tapped my foot along with the beat. The smell of his cologne snuck into my nostrils as I laid back in my chair, remembering the feeling of the fabric of his car seat.

The sky was a nice shade of dark blue and the night's air spilled through the window and blew on my arm. I look over to my left to see the side of his beautifully carved face. The way his little stubble of hair would come in and rest on his chin and cheeks would urge me just to caress it with the back of my hand. I remember feeling uneasy about how I handled things with him a couple nights ago. The look on his face expressed how he truly felt about me and I shut him down because I was scared. Scared that he would soon leave me and I was unsure if I could handle that kind of pain.

"Hey, I just…" He paused. "…I just want to apologize for my actions. I didn't mean to confuse things between us."

"It's fine. You were going through a lot. I understand." Michael switched hands on the steering wheel.

"What I said to you, I did mean. You know me well enough to know that I wouldn't lie to you. In a year I'm graduating High School and I feel like I'm maturing enough to know what I really want out of life." He turned to face me. "And I want you."

My heart dropped. Am I dreaming? Did he really just say that to me?

"Me?" I tried to calm myself down. "Really?"

He faced his attention back on the road and showed off his smirk that I loved so much.

"Really." He reassured while chuckling.

"Michael, I—"

Before I could give him my answer, police sirens went off behind us.

"Shit." Michael breathed.

He reached into his pockets and pulled out a mini bag with a white powder inside. My mouth dropped in shock. He swiftly dumped it under his seat.

"What the hell was that?" I whispered.

"Jade, not now. Just work with me."

Right then, that's where everything changed. Everything happened so fast, I didn't know what to do. Scattered images from that night were misplaced and blurry and I couldn't make out what really happened. The pain that I was longing to never feel, hit me like a heavy truck. Everything that happened from that point on, it felt like a switch went off.

The sound of a gunshot rang in my ears and immediately took me out of my thoughts. I shot up from my daydream and was welcomed to the loud ringing of the bell. I tried to catch my breath as I grabbed my bag and headed to the door. Ms. Collins stopped me before I could complete my exit.

"Are you alright?" Ms. Collins questioned.

"Yeah, I'm fine." I reassured through heavy breaths. She gave me a look.

"Jade, you know I can see right through you. It's not a problem to come talk to me."

I know Ms. Collins is trying to be there for me but some things she just wouldn't understand.

"Trust me, I'm fine. I have to get to my next class. I'll see you on Monday."

Before Ms. Collins could say anything else, I walked out of the classroom.

FOUR

TRUE COLORS

Throughout the entire school day, I could not focus. My mind kept racing back to what I thought about in my first period along with what happened in the morning. I heard my name being called from behind me and I turned around to see who it was. I saw Connor run over to me as my face twisted in disgust.

"Hey." He greeted while he was out of breath.

I shot him a look.

"What? What's wrong?"

"You have no idea, do you?"

He gave me a clueless look. I licked my teeth out of frustration.

"You didn't see what happened this morning? They spray painted harsh words on my locker claiming I'm some slut because I'm taking you away from your *girlfriend*."

His face became blank as he cleared his throat.

"Jade, they were probably just hazing you—"

"That's the same bullshit you tried to feed me last year but it ended up being true. But, what did I do? I gave you another chance because you promised me you wouldn't do this again!" I shouted.

"Keep your voice down, alright." Connor looked around. "Look, what I said, I meant. I wouldn't do that to you. You're the only girl that I love."

It felt like I've heard this same promise before but this time it wasn't as fulfilling as it used to be. I became fed up and I just knew I was sick and tired of this.

"But, I won't be the only girl that you'll fuck."

His eyes widened with shock as that insult parted my lips. I brushed past him and made my way toward the double doors. Connor repeatedly called my name but I ignored him. I'm so tempted to just walk to Mr. Davis' office and quit the Debate Team but, I can't let everyone down. I've been on the Debate Team for three years and it's a wonderful atmosphere. I'm not going to let Connor take something I take pride in, twist it up, and make it unpleasant for me. I'll be damned if I give him that satisfaction but, I just need some time.

As I opened the door to my house, a cigarette smell slapped me across the face. I scrunched up my nose as I slowly closed the door behind me. The scent revealed the sight of my mom in the kitchen concealed in a massive cloud of smoke. Without hesitation, I decided to sneak past her and make my way into my bedroom but I was unsuccessful.

"Jade? You're home early." My mom commented as she knocked off ash from her cigarette butt.

"Yeah. I decided to not stay for Debate." I answered, dryly.

"Debate?" My mom laughed. "You're really wasting your time up there. All you're doing is arguing back and forth with people."

"I'm used to it because I do that with you all day." I retorted under my breath.

My mom stood up and approached me.

"Excuse me?" My mom breathed as the trail of the cigarette smoke traveled into my face as I pulled my head back, slightly. "Your attitude is the reason why we bump heads so much. You're so ungrateful, you know that? I gave you a roof over your head, clothes on your back, and hell, even gave you a job and you try to sneak past me to not hold a conversation with me?"

I stood there in silence. My mom took notice, rolled her eyes, and plopped back down in her seat.

"Whatever." She said.

"Have you ever taken a step back and viewed the *real* reason why we bump heads so much?" I asked.

My mom continued to pull from her cigarette whilst ignoring me.

"Answer me." I demanded.

"I have, Jade." She answered, simply.

"Then, why the hell do you—"

She stood up once more.

"You better watch your mouth! Who the hell do you think you're talking to?" My mom interrupted. She slammed her cigarette into the ashtray and placed her two hands on the small of her back. "You must've lost your damn mind talking to me like that. I don't care how those white people down at your school talk to their parents, you're not about to bring that into this household and disrespect me."

I furrowed my eyebrows together.

"Wow. That's really low. You never gave me a real reason on how I'm disrespecting you. You just assume that to have an excuse to not talk to me. I come home half the time and you are not even here! You never spend time with me to get to know me as a person. You wouldn't even know I was in Debate until you accidentally read the letter that they mailed home."

"While I'm not here, what the hell do you think I'm doing, Jade? Playing hopscotch with my friends? No! I'm trying to provide for you and pay for that high and mighty school by myself! Don't stand here and make me out as a bad person because I'm just trying to help you—"

"Because you feel the need to because you have a title as a mother when that shouldn't be the case!" Silence took a seat in my mom's chair and observed us. The chilling feeling of our altercation left us speechless. I took a deep breath. "You know what, I'm not trying to argue with you. I had a long day and I just need some rest."

I tried to brush past her but unfortunately she grabbed my arm.

"Don't walk away from me." She threatened.

"What are you going to do?" I taunted.

She slapped me across the face. My right cheek stung as tears welled in my eyes. I gave her a look.

Regret instantly hit her as she tried to shake it off. She took a seat.

"That's the exact outcome I expected." A tear streamed down my face. "Wow. I love provoking people because it shows their true colors. You definitely gave me insight on yours."

My mom took a fresh cigarette from the pack and quickly lit it.

"Get out of my face." She spat as she blew smoke in my direction.

I clenched my jaw to prevent harsh words from spilling out of my mouth. Just let it go, Jade. I walked into my room, shut my bedroom door, and landed onto my bed. I stared at my ceiling and watched the lights from the cars on the street pour into my bedroom ceiling. The tear was so cold against my cheek as it dampened my pillow. I turned to my side. My eyelids grew heavy and before I knew it, I fell asleep.

FIVE

RECURRING IMAGES

I shifted uneasily in my seat as my eyes wandered over to the rear view mirror. I viewed Michael having a heated conversation with the police officer as the officer's body language shouted that he wasn't trying to hear what Michael had to say. I couldn't make out what words were being exchanged but I knew it wasn't pleasant. My breathing increased. This situation can go in many directions and I just hope that Michael doesn't get into trouble. I watched intensely.

Shock ripped through me as the officer whipped his flashlight across Michael's face. I immediately got out of the car without thinking and made my way over to them. I stood in between the two.

"What the hell is going on? What are you doing?" I shouted.

I couldn't see the officer's face due to the darkness of the night's sky.

"I suggest you get back in that car." The officer taunted as he drew closer to me.

Fear replaced my shock. I was lost for words and my mind went blank. I looked down at Michael to see him holding the side of his bruised face.

"Now!" The officer shouted as he pushed me.

As I began to walk towards the car, I heard shuffling behind me. I quickly turned around to see Michael on the officer's back. It felt like everything was going in slow motion. I couldn't move. I saw the officer reach for his gun and I couldn't part my lips to warn Michael. The officer managed to knock Michael off of his back and immediately wielded his gun. My eyes grew wide.

"You should've just complied, boy." The officer spat as he pulled the trigger.

Every single breath became uneasy. Every emotion clung to my heart. Every body part shook. I kneeled down to Michael. I looked up with pure anger in my eyes towards the officer. He didn't say a word. It took every part of me to not attack him. I didn't want to be his next victim. The officer's next move was just to leave. He hopped right into his police cruiser and drove off like nothing happened. I searched for my phone. A piece of me broke when I realized that Michael was already gone. I need someone to help me. Help him. Who can you call when the police are out of control?

I landed my fingers onto his eyelids and slowly closed them. Instead of me bawling my eyes out for the loss of my best friend, I felt hatred. I was angry at everyone and everything. I balled up my fist and slammed it onto the ground while screaming Michael's name.

I shot up from my sleep and looked around, anxiously. It's still dark outside. I swung my legs off the side of the bed and wiped my face with my hands. I took a deep breath.

It's been a year since Michael left this earth. Not a day goes by without me thinking about what could've been. I remember telling Regina what happened and she went ballistic on me. She believed that I could've saved him but when somebody is in that situation, it happens so quick and I don't believe anybody's mental state could properly digest what was actually going on. Especially at the age of sixteen. I walked over to my desk and opened my laptop. I opened the Melanin website and clicked the edit tool. I took a deep breath and wrote:

To all the casualties of wrong doings, I shed my tears for you. I've been receiving a lot of messages from families and friends about them losing the ones they love to authority and power and I genuinely feel your pain. I've been through the same hurt as you all. The reason why I'm doing what I do on this website is to shed light on problems that are so overlooked in the African American society. Over 32 African American men were shot and killed by police officers just in the span of the new year of 2019. Just imagine how many more lives would be taken later in the year or how many additions are now that just aren't documented. It's time we open our eyes. We need to make a stand, and we need to make a damn good one. Starting tomorrow, it's going to be a new day. Look out for way more exposure on those dirty cops that need a little wash.

-    Yours truly, Anonymous.

I hit submit and watched the numbers grow. I scrolled through the comment section and read people's reactions.

"Is this a threat?" One person wrote.

"Authority and power? They can get away with anything. What can us as a people do? Absolutely nothing." Another person wrote.

I rolled my eyes and leaned back in my chair. I just want my website to be something that'll take a chunk out of this big problem and lessen it. I'm tired of scrolling through website reports about another black man or woman shot down, killed, raped, or even abused by our so called average heroes. This has been going on for far too long. Somebody has to do something and have that commitment to stand by it. Not just post about it on their social media for likes.

I made a new tab on my computer and searched up Jackson, Mississippi's policemen in the area. I haven't found out who is behind Michael's murder yet. I don't recall any facial feature on the officer. I just know he's an older guy by his voice. I scrolled through different pictures of the officers in Mississippi. Nobody is standing out to me. I closed my eyes and tried to place myself back at the scene. I need something from that night to guide me toward the identity of the officer. The license plate. I vaguely remember the letters and numbers from the police cruiser. I grabbed a sheet of paper and wrote down what I recalled from that night.

I viewed the sheet while biting my lip in deep thought. I searched up the license plate number on the internet along with the tag of my area. I scrolled through, endlessly. It's like trying to find a needle in the world's biggest haystack.

I spotted a police cruiser with most of the letters and numbers I wrote down on its license plate. I wrote down the license plate below the one written down before. I quickly placed my attention back on the laptop and clicked the picture of the cruiser. I scrolled through the description to see if there's an owner attached. Of course, the website didn't provide information on who was driving the cruiser.

"Shit." I breathed as I swiftly kicked the desk.

This is so frustrating! How can I find this officer? Everything is documented when it comes down to police work. I just need to get my hands on a few documents from a year ago. But how? No way is the easy way. I could always go into the police department and ask who was driving the cruiser the day of the incident. But, that just seems suspicious. Plus, they wouldn't be dumb enough to just tell me who the officer is without question. I need to keep my low profile contained.

Michael, on the other hand, was a man of discretion. He didn't let me in on a lot of things that were troubling him. I remember him throwing a small bag of drugs underneath his seat the day of the incident. Ever since his brother was shot and killed, he stayed away from all of that bullshit his brother was in. This isn't adding up. What made him go out and buy that drug? Was he selling it? But, for what? How does this all tie up to a police officer killing him, wrongly? It seemed like they were having a heated discussion before a bullet was shot. It also felt like that wasn't their first encounter either. I need insight about a lot more things that would potentially help me get a lead on this case.

SIX

TOXICITY

I placed the rag inside of a wet cup and swiftly wiped the sides. The glass shined once I assigned it next to the rest of the dried dishes. I let the warm water run over my hands as I let out a breath. My mind is all over the place. I have so many things unfinished and it's driving me insane. I picked up another dirty dish. I suddenly felt someone's presence behind me which caused me to turn around. I saw my mother propped up against the wall with her arms folded. I tried to understand what she is feeling as I studied her facial expressions. I want to be prepared for what words were going to escape out her mouth. Considering that my mom is very guarded when it comes down to her emotions that becomes damn near impossible. She doesn't let her emotions swell up and crowd her to the point where she can't breathe. She buries it and goes through the world not giving a damn. I could say she is strong but if I was her, I wouldn't let those emotions harvest and fester. It can tear someone up to no point of return. No wonder why she's the asshole that she is but, I sympathize for her.

"You have a visitor. Tell your little friend to not come around here because this is your line of work."

I kept quiet. I dried my hands on the sides of my apron and attempted to walk past my mom but she landed her hand on my shoulder. I looked up at her.

"I'm still waiting on my apology from last night." She mentioned as she went back to folding her arms.

"Like you said, this is my line of work. This is not the time nor the place to be discussing this." I retorted. She licked her teeth out of frustration.

"That smart ass mouth isn't going to get you anywhere in life."

I rolled my eyes as I let that insult roll off of my shoulders. I brushed past her. I began to look around to see who my potential visitor was. My eyes immediately recognized Connor standing by the door with a smile on his face. I hung my apron on the coat rack and approached him. I have to make sure that I am mentally prepared for the bullshit that Connor is going to try and feed to me. I really don't want to make a scene in my mother's diner. I approached him. Connor hesitantly pulled me into a hug as I pulled away. Connor took notice and made a face.

"I didn't have to come here and make amends with you, Jade." He spoke.

"Then why did you? I made it very clear to you on how I felt. Why are you coming back?" I asked.

"The answer is simple. I love you. You know if it wasn't for me, you wouldn't be standing here right now."

My stomach dropped. It felt hard for me to breathe. Connor knows I become vulnerable when he brings up my past. Especially, the specific time he is referring to.

"Connor, don't bring that up to me again." I finally spoke.

My face became hot and I just knew tears would follow afterward. I fought back my tears as I rubbed my arm up and down. Connor grabbed my arm and decided to bring me close to him.

"Jade, I care for you too much to just let you go like this."

My eyebrows furrowed in confusion as I looked at his hand resting on my arm. I looked back up to him through narrow eyes.

"Get your pathetic ass out of my diner."

Connor's eyes narrowed as his fist balled up with anger. He got close to my ear and whispered things I never thought he would say. Anger arose in my chest as I immediately walked over to a customer's table, grabbed a glass of their water, and threw it on his face. Connor's eyes widened in shock as water dripped from his face. I threw the glass onto the floor which caused the glass to shatter into a million pieces. I ripped my apron off of my torso and stormed out of the diner.

I heard my name being shouted from behind me as I kept walking further and further away. I wasn't trying to hear what anyone had to say to me at the moment. I dug into my pocket in search for my phone. Once I found it, I dialed Regina's number and told her my location hoping she was available to come pick me up.

SEVEN

REKINDLING

An awkward silence spread around in the car. Regina tapped her fingers on the top part of her steering wheel as her other hand rested on her lap. She snuck a few glances at me. Once I caught her eyes staring into mine, I gave her an awkward smile. Regina smiled back and landed her hand onto the radio to change the station. A familiar song came on as she turned up the volume.

"You remember this? This used to be our song!" Regina announced as she bobbed her head to the music.

A genuine smile spread across my face. I began to mouth the words. Regina took notice and immediately started shouting the lyrics from the top of her lungs. I joined in. For the first time in a long time, I felt happy. This reminded me of the days when it was more simple and more fun. I began to bask in the ambiance of it all.

The song soon faded away leaving the car filled with our laughter. Regina reached for the volume and turned it down.

"That song is a classic." She commented while chuckling. "If you really want to hear some good music, you should come with me to this house party tonight."

"A house party? You know that really isn't my scene."

"It used to be. Come on, Jade. How bad can it be? There's going to be free drinks, amazing music, and plus boys are going to be there. You need to branch out and get out of your comfort zone." Regina stated.
I weighed my thoughts.

"Okay, hypothetically speaking, if I go to this house party I wouldn't have anything to wear."

Regina looked both left and right before she made a sharp U-turn. My cheek squished onto the window as Regina jolted her car in between oncoming traffic. The car straightened back out once she found her place on the road. I flung back upright and glared at Regina.

"What the hell are you doing?" I shouted.

"I'm taking you shopping."

We walked inside to be greeted by the workers of the store. Regina approached one of the workers and started to describe what outfit she was looking for. As she was browsing around with the worker, I timidly looked around. There are so many clothes here. I doubt that I'll walk out with something I will actually like.

I made my way towards a few dresses aligned against the wall. I aimlessly searched through them. I don't know what outfit I would wear to this occasion. I just know that I don't want to be too undressed or too overdressed. I also would like something that's comfortable but it also looks good on me. A lot of these clothing items don't quite fit those criterias.

I stopped looking once my hand landed onto a dress that caught my eye. I fingered the edge of the soft fabric. It was a black suede dress that looked like it'll stop on my upper thigh. I took it off of the hanger and placed it against my chest. I stood in the mirror. I caressed the dress while tilting my head to the side.

"Jade, I—" Regina stopped once she saw me admiring the dress.

I looked at her through the mirror.

"I want this one." I said with a smile.

"You sure? There's plenty of more dresses here. You shouldn't settle for the first one you see."

I turned around to face her.

"I'm sure."

"Alright. Go try it on and see how it looks on you. I'll be outside with some accessories."

I nodded my head and walked into the fitting room. I went into a stall and closed the door behind me. I stripped out of my jeans and shirt and placed them on the bench next to me. I removed the dress off of the hanger and started to put it onto my body. The dress hugged my hips and exposed my curves that I didn't even know I had. I turned around to see my behind protruding. I made a face of approval while I viewed myself in the mirror. I walked out of the dressing room and stood in front of Regina. Regina turned around and once she saw me, her mouth dropped in shock.

"Goddamn! Girl, you better work! Out here serving looks!" She shouted as she circled around me.

I smiled while looking down. Regina held up the accessories she picked out. I viewed them with my head tilting to the side. The accessories were silver which complimented the dress, perfectly.

"It's beautiful."

"I know right. I shop for a living." She joked.

I let out a laugh and hugged her.

"You really don't need to do all of this for me. I could pay for it myself." I mentioned as I let her go.

"No, I told you I got it. Plus, this is the first time we're hanging out in what, a year? It's the least I could do."

I let out a breath.

"You're right." I smiled. "You got all of this."

Regina playfully hit my shoulder as she joined me in a big laugh.

EIGHT

OMINOUS

Bodies constantly bumped into each other as they swayed back and forth in rhythm with the music. The vibrations were so strong, you could feel it persuade your heart to beat along with it. The different colored lights glistened on people's sweaty foreheads and arms. The atmosphere felt somewhat ominous. Like something was urging me to call it a night and just go home. I shook my head in disbelief. I'm always thinking myself out of having fun. You know what? I am going to enjoy myself tonight. All of my worries and all of my stress are going to take a trip out of the window. But, this gut-wrenching feeling kept tugging at me. I'm getting way too many weird vibes from this place.

Regina tugged at my arm to take me over to the table where they were serving drinks. I shrugged my shoulders at Regina while looking down. A couple strands of my hair fell into my left eye as I brushed it off with my finger. I'm definitely not used to having my hair lay comfortably at the sides of my face. I find it too distracting. I noticed that my dress was beginning to ride up. I reached for the end of my dress until Regina stopped me. She got close to my ear.

"Leave your dress alone!" She shouted over the music.

"It's moving up my thigh!" I responded.

"Exactly. Let it."

Regina laughed as she began to pour both of us drinks. She handed me the red plastic cup and held hers in the air.

"To new beginnings!" Regina said while tapping her cup against mine.

I watched Regina plug her nose while taking a huge gulp of her drink. I furrowed my eyebrows together while twirling the liquid inside of my cup. She let out a breath once she finished chugging down her drink. She glared at me.

"You still have some left?"

I gave her a blank stare. Regina tapped the bottom of my cup and crossed her arms. I took a deep breath before I let the liquor travel down my throat. It stung the walls of my throat as I began to lightly cough. Regina shook her head.

"Damn. I'm going to have to get you drunk by the end of this night so you can have some *real* fun."

Regina grabbed my hand and pulled me towards the middle of a huge crowd. She began to dance to the beat as she looked around. I awkwardly swayed back and forth. Regina took notice and placed my arms into her grasps. She moved me like I was her puppet while she was the master. I laughed as I began to shed away all of my timidness. I started to dance on my own.

A smile parted my lips as I began to let myself be myself. Mount High really altered my character. Due to the bullying, I'm always reserved around people. I never let my inner self come out because I feared judgement and ridicule. I would do that all the time to the point where I almost forgot who I was. I'm sort of glad Regina drug me out here.

Different songs poured out of the speaker causing Regina to sway her hips back and forth. She constantly went to and from the dancing area and table filled with refreshments. She poured herself drinks to the point where I couldn't keep up with her. A tall man soon approached Regina. He instantly landed his hands onto her thighs and whispered into her ear. Regina landed her hand onto his cheek and laughed. She looked over to me.

"Jade, I would like you to meet Ricky. He's the one that put together this wonderful party." Regina stated.

Ricky reached out his hand towards me. I shook his hand.

"It's nice to meet you. I'm Jade."

"Likewise." Ricky said as he placed his hand back to its original position.

Ricky spoke something onto Regina that I couldn't comprehend. From the looks of it, it wasn't pleasant. I scrunched up my face in confusion. Ricky soon grabbed Regina by her arm and motioned for her to go towards the back of the house. Regina looked over to me and instructed me to follow behind her.

All three of us were pushing through the crowd of people until we were greeted by stairs that led downward. Ricky shifted his eyeballs downward then back at Regina. We began to make our way downstairs. Green carpet rested on the floor as wood panels hugged the walls. A pool table was in the middle of the floor as a couch filled with people rested on the side. People stood against the wall like a vine that grew on an old building. I noticed that a pistol rested on their waist as they side eyed Regina and I.

Ricky pressed his hands onto the pool table and glared at us. I looked over to Regina to see her full attention on him. What the hell is going on?

"Regina, baby. You made a drop last week and only paid me ten percent of that money. You've worked for me for three years and we never had this issue. You've seen what happened to people that don't pay their debt on time. Do you want to be that person?" Ricky spoke.

"No, sir. Look, I have the money but I wasn't able to bring it tonight. I was just going to show my friend a good time before—"

"What you're saying to me is that business doesn't come first?" Ricky interrupted.

"No, sir. I was going to—"

Ricky held his hand up. He approached Regina and delivered a fresh slap across her face. Regina flung to the floor as Ricky shouted at her to get up. My eyes widened in shock. I noticed in the corner of my eye that someone was staring me down. I connected eyes with him and he kept moving his iris around like he's signaling me to do something. I furrowed my eyebrows in confusion. Ricky held her face and got close to her.

"I have really grown fond of you and what you have down to contribute to my business. But, this little petty shit is going to get you killed. I expect my money to be in my hand by tomorrow with no excuses and not a penny out of place. You got that?"

Regina shook her head in fear. Ricky clenched his jaw.

"I don't understand head movements. God gave you mouth so speak to me." Ricky demanded.

"Y-yes. I understand." Regina trembled.

Ricky smoothed her dress with his hands and moved her hair back into place. He landed his hand onto her shoulder and looked at me.

"Jade, right?"

My stomach dropped.

"Yes."

"You don't remember me?" Ricky began to approach me. My eyes caught onto the guy trying to signal me again but Ricky held my face so I could have his full attention. "My little trooper."

Oh shit! Shit, shit, shit. I do slightly remember him. The scar that rested on his left eye made his appearance less recognizable to me. My breathing became uneasy as I felt his breath rest on my neck.

"Yes." I managed to say.

He let me go as I held my chin. Ricky circled around me and made a sound of approval.

"You grew up nicely. Do you need a job? I have something for you that you will fit perfectly in."

Regina shook her head, no.

"No. I'm fine." I answered.

"Ricky? Are we dismissed?" Regina asked.

Ricky turned around to face Regina. I saw his fist ball up as he clenched his jaw. The guy in the corner that was signaling me reached for his gun and fired a bullet in the ceiling. Everyone got down, including me. I heard screams from upstairs followed by several footsteps. The guy approached me, grabbed my arm and grabbed Regina's. We ran upstairs as we heard shouting from behind us. The guy handed Regina a pistol as they both wielded it in their defense.

"You got your car?" He asked Regina.

"Yeah, parked around back."

"What the hell is going on?" I shouted.

A bullet whizzed past my arm as Regina pulled me to the side. I looked towards the damaged wall due to the bullet. I placed my attention back onto the guy who was looking for the back door. Once he found it, we all made our exit. A few guys with huge guns stood in front of us. They were about to aim but Regina and the guy penetrated them with their bullets. I stood there in shock. Regina took notice and tugged me along towards the car.

We all got inside as the guy drove Regina's car down the street. My heart was beating so fast it felt like it was going to fall out of my chest.

"Can someone please give me an explanation on what the hell is going on?" I shouted once more.

"Jade, calm down. This wasn't supposed to go down like this—"

"Like what? A fucking shootout? You could've gotten me killed!"

"Oh, please. They couldn't have hit you if they tried. Look, Jade, I'm sorry. I know we were supposed to enjoy this party but I really didn't know it would go down like this."

"W-what? What are you talking about? You owe Ricky money so just pay him! You would rather go through all of this for possibly a hundred dollars?" I questioned.

"Try two thousand." The guy interjected.

"Two thousand dollars, Regina? Is selling dope that damn serious?"

"Yes, it is. Especially with Ricky. It's a system that you wouldn't understand." Regina answered.

"Try me."

Regina looked at the guy driving. The guy gave a doubtful look. Regina looked back onto the road.

"Fine. Think of it this way. Ricky is the manager of this business. He gives us the supplies to sell and we give him thirty percent of what we made. Now, that thirty percent gets sent to the owner of this business. Now, if the owner isn't happy, then Ricky isn't happy which means the little puppets they have on the strings get cut. Understand?" She explained.

"Do you know who the owner is?" I asked.

"Nobody knows. We just know that this business is more complicated than we thought. I wanted to get out of this game for so long but once you're in it, you're *in* it. Death is the only way out and I'm not going out like that."

I looked out of the window. My mind began to race.

"If you've been in this *game* for so long, what really happened to Michael's brother?" I asked.

Regina looked at the guy as he took a deep breath.

"Montell, Michael's brother, tried to do the same thing we did. He had a debt he couldn't pay off so he ran. They found him at a bar and killed him on the spot. He was the nicest guy I've met since I've been slangin'.

He didn't deserve what they did to him. Montell was smart. He had it going for him but reality set in and he tried to keep his family straight. That's why he pressured Michael to stay in the books and not worry about the real shit. But, eventually, that all faded away." The guy stated.

"What do you mean faded away?"

"Once Montell died, they found out that he had a younger brother. The debt passed onto him and that's when Michael got into the game."

That's why Michael had that small plastic bag in his pocket. He was selling drugs to pay off the debt. I leaned back in my seat.

"Before he got shot, he was having a heated conversation with an officer. The officer said something to him before he pulled the trigger." I mentioned.

Regina turned around in her seat and glared at me.

"What did he say?" She asked.

"You should've just complied."

Regina looked at the guy and began to rub her forehead.

"This is deeper than I thought. It's *regularized* for black men to be killed off by a police officer so I didn't think anything different about Michael's death. He was a hot head but not to the point where he would put himself in a position to get himself killed. No way would the middle class people prey on someone without a good reason." The guy said.

"Middle class people? Speak English to me!" I demanded.

"Dirty cops are in this system too. They're the important people, so to speak. They order the supplies under the orders of the owner. I'm just uneasy at the thought of a dirty cop handling Ricky's business. From what I know, that isn't in their job description." He responded.

"So, they just get information about the drugs and give it to Ricky to be dispersed in the neighborhood? But, some cops go out and sell it themselves."

"That's not true. Some cops are selling it to minors to possibly start their own business and then there would be two businesses that'll eventually turn against each other like Blood and Crip. Nobody wants that war." He spoke. The guy slammed on his breaks and turned around with his gun pointed at me. Regina shouted his name as I absorbed this newly acquired information. "How do you know that?"

My breathing increased.

"Tell me!" Andre insisted.

"I-I tried to find the cop behind Michael's murder but in the process I've created a website to put justice to cops that need it. I hack into neighborhood cameras and watch the shady shit that goes on at night and report about it to get citizens attention."

"You are the creator of that Melanin website?" He asked.

"Yes. I'm trying to shed light on this issue but I didn't know it was this connected. In all actuality, I'm just focused on finding that officer while delivering a message."

Andre looked back onto the road and began to drive again.

"Let's just..." He paused. "...get you home."

NINE

PRACTICE WHAT YOU PREACH

The loud ringing of the bell clung to my ears as I scrunched up my face in annoyance. Everyone began to dash out of the classroom leaving me the last student in the room. I began to gather my things. Ms. Collins stood in front of the door to prevent me from leaving.

"This is getting quite repetitive." I murmured.

"It isn't if it's for good reason." She responded. "Why haven't you turned in your assignment?"

"I didn't get around to it." I admitted.

"It's not like you to ever miss an assignment. Are you sure everything is alright?"

The events that occurred on Saturday rushed back to me like an avalanche. I began to rub my arm up and down to prevent me from showing any emotion to allow Ms. Collins to question me further.

"Everything's fine. I was just busy working." I lied. She gave me a look.

"Okay. I expect that assignment on my desk tomorrow, understood?"

I nodded my head.

"You're dismissed."

I let out a breath while walking out of the classroom. I have to make sure that Ms. Collins is off of my back so she can be the least of my worries. I began to walk towards the cafeteria. The dirty blonde hair girl nudged me with her shoulder once I entered inside. Her group of friends laughed at me as I adjusted my bag back onto my shoulder. I gave them a look. The girl took notice and stopped in her tracks. She faced me. Her bright blue eyes were filled with hatred. I don't understand why I am such a target at this school.

"You got a problem?" She asked as she tilted her head to the side.

I kept quiet. I really don't need to be dealing with this. I just want to eat.

"It seems to me that she has a problem." She announced as her friends laughed their heads off.

Everyone in the cafeteria turned their attention onto us. Some were sitting in anticipation while others were provoking the girl to hit me. I looked around to see if any type of authority figure was here to stop this nonsense. I noticed that the lunch ladies stood at their posts while ignoring the situation. I swiftly rolled my eyes.

One of her friends grabbed my bag from off of my shoulder. I tried to grab it back but her other friend stood in front of her.

"Check and see what the freak has in her bag." The girl demanded with a smirk.

I watched as her friend pulled everything out of my bag. My papers, books, bus card, and dignity. My items were all laid onto the floor as they trampled it with their expensive shoes.

"Why are you doing this?" I finally spoke.

The girl widened her eyes in shock. It was like she convinced herself that I couldn't speak.

"Why not? You do like to sleep with other girls' boyfriends. You're just a disgrace, I mean, look at you. You're hideous." She taunted.

I took a deep breath. I feel so humiliated and belittled and for what? A lie she is trying to cover up because she's guilty of those things? Or maybe, because of the color of my skin? The uniqueness in my personality? No more. I will not be ostracized because I am different. I tell people all the time on my website to stand up for their rights and it's about time I shove my own encouragement down my throat.

"Don't try and pin your insecurities on me. Connor was my boyfriend since the beginning of my Junior year. The infidelity started once your fast ass transferred into this school. I'm not going to pin that allegation on you but it's a nine out of ten chance that you were the one sleeping around. Hell, I even heard there is footage of you trying to get a good grade out of a teacher but not in the ways of tutoring. Who is the slut now?" I stated.

The entire cafeteria filled with silence. Some students stood up to get a better view of the confrontation. The dirty blond haired girl had a blank stare. In the corner of my eye I saw Connor walk in. Our eyes connected but I quickly looked away. Before I could intentionally react, the girl slapped me across the face. I flung into one of her friends as she shoved me onto the ground. Their shoes connected to my ribs as I gasped for air. The dirty blonde hair girl pushed through her friends and looked down at me. She grabbed my shirt and pulled me towards her.

"Don't ever disrespect me like that again. You're not even on my level to talk to me, nigger." She spat as she connected her fist onto my face.

I felt my lip split as my head landed onto the ground. I covered my head as the group of girls continued to jump me. I heard shouting from the far end of the cafeteria which made the girls stop hitting me. They immediately dispersed and took their seats like nothing happened. Tears welled in my eyes as pain lived throughout my body. I curled up into a ball to try and stop some of the agonizing pain. I saw someone hover above me but my vision was blurred due to the wetness of my eyes.

"Are you alright?" A familiar voice spoke upon me.

I couldn't get a word out of my mouth. I was too busy trying not to pass out due to my injuries. The person grabbed my arm and slowly lifted me up to my feet. They soon slung one of my arms onto their shoulders and led me out of the cafeteria.

My mom burst through the door frantically and looked around.

"What happened?" She shouted as she looked at my bruises.

My mom kneeled down in front of me and held my chin to observe my face. I moved my face to the side and brushed her off.

"Well, Mrs. Morris—"

"Miss." She corrected.

The principle cleared his throat.

"Ms. Morris, your child was involved in a fight and the teacher that happened to walk in couldn't make out who Jade was fighting. The person quickly blended in with the crowd and all the teacher saw was Jade bleeding on the floor."

"Ain't no way in hell that Jade could've fought one person. Do you see her bruises? She's been jumped!" My mom shouted as she stood upright.

"Mom—"

"Jade, I'm talking." She interrupted.

I sat back in my chair and heaved out a breath. I listened as my mom continued to mouth off instead of listening to what the principal had to say. This issue could've been resolved hours ago if I just told them who jumped me. I don't want to have the mere satisfaction of reporting the girls to authority, I'd rather get even. Now, it's a personal thing. The dirty blonde haired girl messed up when she let the word *nigger* come out of her mouth. She doesn't know who she is messing with. Does she know that I expose people on a daily basis and I'm damn good at it? Oh, nobody knows. I guess this is just going to make this a lot more interesting.

I looked out of the window as buildings and different structures passed us by. The different bumps in the road caused us to sway back and forth. I fingered the bottom of my busted lip with my eyes narrowed. The reflection from the window mirrored my face as I looked away due to the constant reminder of humiliation.

"See where that smart ass mouth got you. I tried to warn you." My mom chastised.

I scrunched up my face as I turned my body towards her.

"Are you serious? Out of all times, this is when you want to start an argument with me?"

"Oh, please. You think I get anything out of this? I'm not trying to start anything, I was just simply stating a point. You need to start listening to your mother or shit like this is going to keep happening." She responded.

I let out an aggravated sigh as I turned my body towards the window. Sometimes not saying anything speaks a thousand words.

TEN

REMODELING

Days passed by like months considering how long they dragged out. I always look forward to a new day because in my opinion, a new day means that you can just start over and become a better you. But, being me, it's more complex than the average person. I'm constantly living one day over each moment of my life. I can't shake the memories I had from that night nor constant reminders of how much he impacted my desire to live. Looking Michael in the eyes and standing alongside Regina just made me want to be better. It made me want to strive towards my passion so we can all fill that fantasy of living together in a big house like we've always wanted. As kids, we weren't thinking of possibly getting married to someone and having that dream crumble down. We just looked forward to the happy ending. It's funny that once you get older the less creative and thought seeking you are when life takes a seat onto your shoulder. It's true what they say, life's a bitch.

My mom wouldn't allow me to go back to school for a couple of days. She wanted all of the bruising to simmer down so I wouldn't attract as much attention to myself. But, little does she know, the whole fight was posted on social media for everyone to see. Everything in me was urging to expose the dirty blonde hair girl but I've realized that I wouldn't be any better than what she is. I don't want to stoop down to her level and lose my sense of self. Instead, I'll just revamp my image and show her how unbothered I am. She can manipulate my self worth and attack my body but one thing she can't do is take anything away from my beautiful soul.

I crept into my mom's bedroom and looked around carefully. I had to make sure she left the house so I could *borrow* some of her money to make changes to my hair. I've never gone to the hair salon before. My mom would always sit me in between her legs as she would do different braiding styles in my hair. As fun as all the tugging and pulling went, it soon stopped once I hit high school. Like I've stated before, she views me as a young adult that should fend for herself. Now, I'm just stuck with ponytails with a headband resting above. Something has to change.

As I opened the front door of my apartment building, I saw Andre walking in my direction. He soon stopped once we made eye contact. I furrowed my eyebrows together while closing the door behind me.

"What are you doing here?" I asked, concerned.

Andre licked his lips while looking over my shoulder. He soon placed his attention back on me.

"We need to talk."

I crossed my arms and pressed my back onto the wall awaiting for him to speak.

"Not here. You never know who is listening. That's why I came here so we can discuss this in your house." He stated.

"Look, you're going to have to schedule this *talk* later because I have somewhere else to be." I responded.

"I'll come with."

I scrunched up my face.

"What? No, you can't come with me—"

"Why not? What's so important that you can't have this quick discussion with me?" Andre interrupted.

"It's none of your damn business. I barely know you, okay? There's no reason why you should be coming to my house especially under the circumstances. Now, I'd advise you to step away from my door before I call the cops."

Andre let out a chuckle.

"The cops? Now, you know you don't fuck with twelve." Andre stopped smirking once he realized that I was serious. "Alright, fine. I'll be back here around seven o'clock. Don't make me wait."

Andre began to walk away from me.

"Just don't come back!" I shouted.

Andre stuck up two fingers and waved them while laughing to himself. I let out a sigh as I clenched my jaw in frustration. I don't understand why he has to come to my apartment to talk to me but it does make me curious as to what the reason is. I need to stop thinking about that interaction with him, I have things to get done.

I hopped off of the bus while looking left and right. I quickly read the sign above the hair salon. *Curls and Care*. A bell sounded as I opened the door which caused everyone to turn their heads at me. I awkwardly stood there as everyone started to stir back up their conversations.

"What's your name, sweetie?" A lady standing behind a chair asked me.

"Jade." I answered.

"Alright, Jade. I'll be right with you. Go ahead and have a seat."

I sat next to an old lady as she flipped through a magazine. I anxiously tapped my foot as I looked up at the television screen in the corner of the room. A lady doing her client's hair turned up the volume.

"A police officer shot and killed an unarmed African American male who was driving over the speed limit. Reports say that he was pulled over by the cop who allegedly pulled him out of the vehicle after he wasn't cooperating. The video surfaced a couple days after the incident and here is what took place. Take a look."

I watched as the officer leaned on the guy's car as he was talking to the individual through a cracked opened window. The cop soon lost his composure and yelled at the man. His shouting was inaudible so I didn't understand the officer's frustration. The guy in the car knew that it was a life or death situation so he decided to stay in the vehicle. The officer soon broke the window, opened the car door, and pulled him out of the car. The video was cut off due to the shooting being too graphic for the average eye. This footage made my skin crawl. It's a slim chance that the guy and his family will earn justice. The officer will probably be on paid leave like every other cop that had an incident similar to this. It's sickening. Why not give justice where it needs to be served?

"It's crazy how numb I am to this kind of news. This is happening everywhere." The client said.

I shook my head in disbelief.

"We shouldn't be accustomed to this kind of behavior. Police should be preventing these things from happening. If an average person did this to this guy, they would've quickly arrested him without a doubt. But, it's okay if a police officer does it just because he got angry and his actions are justified because he's wearing a goddamn badge? Hell no, that's not right." I interjected.

Everyone began to agree with me. The client sat up straighter in her chair.

"We all know that, that isn't right. But, you have no idea how much power we have compared to the justice system. It's slim to none. We can't do jack shit about this. We just let it happen. You know how many protests and walkouts we have had in these past few years? A ton. It ain't change nothing. This has been going on for as long as I can remember. The only thing that *changed* is that people have phones to record this and let it be known what's really going down in these streets."

This argument seemed familiar to me. She reminded me of a comment that was posted on my Melanin website. It's a chance that she was the one who posted it. I need to make sure I don't say something that Anonymous would say.

"I understand that but that doesn't mean we just give up. Just because our protests and our plea for our rights is not going our way doesn't mean we just hold our hands up and step back. We as a community can all step up and do something. Most of you all are just fucking lazy."

The entire beauty salon became quiet. The client held up her hand. The lady that was working on her hair stopped and the client stood up. She approached me as I looked up at her.

"Let me make this clear as possible to you because you're probably too young to understand. We - black people - can't do shit." She began to smooth out my shirt with her hands. "Now, you sit there and let us grown folks talk."

"Get your hands off of me." I said in a hushed tone.

"What is your little ass going to do, honey? You better learn how to respect your elders." She said as she placed her hand on top of my head and petted me.

"Alright, that's enough, Cynthia. This is a family friendly salon. Everyone is open to talk and they're entitled to their own opinions. I don't want any fighting or bickering in here. If you all are going to do that, take that mess outside."

Cynthia gave me a look before she returned back to her chair. The lady behind the chair motioned for me to take a seat.

"My name is Tasha, I will be doing your hair for today. Is there anything you would like to get done to it?" The lady introduced.

I looked at myself in the mirror and quickly debated on what style would perfect an image in my mind. I motioned for Tasha to bend down to me which she did. I got close to her ear and whispered the style that I had in mind. Tasha straightened back up and started to observe my hair.

"This style is going to look perfect on you."

ELEVEN

ULTIMATUM

Light beamed onto Andre's face as he looked down at his phone. His thumb constantly scrolled through different images as every picture left Andre more anxious. His left eyebrow raised as he saw me approaching the door. From the looks of Andre, he seems like he's around twenty years of age. His facial structure is very strong considering how fit his body was. His skin tone was a light shade of brown that looked close to the color of caramel. Dimples engraved the side of his cheeks whenever he would make a slight movement with his mouth while his dark brown eyes pierced into my soul. Whenever I look into Andre's eyes, it intimidates me because I can sense how much hurt and trauma lays behind it. I can tell he shelters his true self away so he would never be vulnerable. I can definitely relate to that. A subtle mustache laid on top of his plump lips as he tucked his bottom lip underneath his top row of teeth.

"That's why you left? For a hair appointment?" Andre questioned.

I rolled my eyes as I unlocked the door. I instructed Andre to shut the door behind him as he walked inside. Luckily, my mom is planning on working late which means Andre has enough time to talk to me about whatever he has on his mind. I took a seat on the couch to be welcomed next to him. A trail of his scent hugged my nose as he kept adjusting his body to get comfortable. Goosebumps rose on my forearms as a shiver sent down my spine. I regained my focus and made eye contact with him.

"What did you want to talk about?" I asked.
Andre took a deep breath.

"I was up all night reflecting on what you told Regina and I the night of the shootout. I understand what you are trying to do but believe it or not, you've got yourself in a predicament I'm sure you can't get out of without our help."

"Excuse me?" I said with my eyebrows furrowed.
Andre landed his elbow onto his knee and caressed his chin.

"It's only a matter of time before those cops you are exposing track down your IP address and murder you. This isn't a game, Jade. You can be a couple steps ahead of them and take out their entire operation, that'll eventually help you and everyone else in the hood. They are given an ultimatum that is basically life or death. I know because I am a product of it. We can't save everybody but we damn sure can save a handful."

Andre explained as he clenched his jaw. "Or, you can sit back and continue what you are doing and get yourself killed. We have a direction and we need to take a step. It's your choice."

Endless possibilities kept replaying in my mind as I tried to focus at the subject at hand. I can't pinpoint what decision I should make. I understand that they are looking out for me but I've been doing this for a little over a year now and I haven't witnessed anything out of the ordinary. What if what he is telling me is true? I don't know Andre that well to read him and understand what his true intentions are. That is what scares me the most about him.

"If I do agree to what you are offering me, what am I actually going to do?" I asked in fear of the answer.

Andre smirked as he licked his lips. He stood up from the couch and faced me. Andre lifted up the side of his shirt which exposed his nicely toned abs and placed a pistol onto the coffee table. I felt my entire body glue to the couch as constant reminders of Michael being shot pressed against my mind. I can't seem to shake the same feeling I felt when I stood and watched, helplessly, as Michael fought for his life. I just feel so guilty and stupid. I tear myself down every single day about the decision I made. It's time for me to step up and start doing something.

"That should give you a hint. I'm not for all of this chit chat. I'm all about getting shit done. We have *something* to do on Friday. Regina will inform you of everything you need to know." Andre explained.

"Wait, I have Debate Finals to attend on that day. I'm not sure I can—"

"It's either you are in or out. Are you sure that Debate is more important than your life?" He mocked. I swallowed hard and kept quiet.

"Like I said before, it's your choice."

Andre began to walk towards the door but stopped once I instructed him to. He turned around to glare at me.

"You forgot your gun." I mentioned.

He let out a chuckle.

"I can't take something that isn't mine." He said as he winked at me.

The door closed behind him as he completed his exit. I looked down at the gun and heard Michael's sweet voice. I racked up the courage to wrap my fingers around the gun's handle. I lifted it up and viewed the pistol. It's crazy that something so small can end up impacting someone's life immensely. I took a deep breath and carried the gun to my room. I placed it into my desk drawer and closed it. For some odd reason, I felt my cheeks become wet as my vision blurred. I didn't even realize that tears were soon falling out of my eyes. Things are starting to change and I am not accustomed to all of this unwanted activity.

A knock landed onto my front door which made my body tense up. That better not be Andre coming back to report to me that he forgot something. I quickly wiped my face and made my way over to the door. As I opened the door, I was welcomed to the sight of Ms. Collins. I furrowed my eyebrows together in confusion.

"Ms. Collins, may I help you?" I asked as I held onto the door.

"I came here to check on you." She clutched her purse as she looked around, anxiously. "Can I come in?"

I opened the door wider so she could step inside. Once she was into the living room area, I closed the door behind me. Freckles laid across her nose. The scattered placement reminded me of looking up at the sky and viewing how many stars littered the night's canvas. Her auburn hair was pulled back tightly in a bun exposing some gray hairs that appeared across her hairline. Her blue eyes gleamed through her thick glasses expressing how awkward she was to be in my presence. She placed her purse onto the coffee table and looked at me, expectantly.

"I told you before, Ms. Collins, there is nothing wrong with me." I spoke as I folded my arms.

"You can say what you want, Jade, but I've noticed a shift in you since the beginning of your Junior year. I haven't seen you smile or even engage in class discussions like you used to do."

"People change." I answered quickly.

"As your English teacher, I am worried about you. Something is just compelling me to help you."

"You really want to help me?" I asked. Ms. Collins swiftly nodded her head. "One thing you can do, is get the hell out of my apartment."

Disappointment washed all over her face as she let out a deep breath. She reached for her purse and approached the door. Ms. Collins stopped walking once she was parallel with me.

"I really hope you get back to your old self. I remember looking into your eyes and seeing how excited you were for your future. Now everything is blurred and corrupted. We need more people like you, Jade. The world right now is changing. If you decide to be that person who steps to the beat of their own drum, people will follow. Be an example to these teenagers — that are also our future — who just need guidance to the right direction. You have something, Jade. Don't lose that and become like everyone else."

I turned my head towards her to view the side of her face. Her eyes were glossy as she quickly wiped her nose.

"I can't be everyone's saint."

Hypocrisy seeped through my skin and corrupted my bloodstream.

Ms. Collins licked her lips as she sniffled.

"You could be."

Ms. Collins completed her exit as I stood in the middle of the room feeling empty. I looked down at the floor. Why does everyone expect so much from me? I can barely take care of myself and she expects me to be an example amongst the youth? I just need to keep a clear mind before I let every little thing get to me. I already feel like a dried up cookie that is starting to crumble apart.

TWELVE

DISPROPORTIONATE OUTCOMES

The floor beneath me blurred as I felt my adrenaline rush throughout my body. The thump of my footsteps bounced off of the hallway walls as I made my way towards the auditorium. I can't believe I lost track of time. I always have so much on my mind that I can barely keep track of my priorities. I burst through the auditorium's double doors as everyone turned their heads towards me. Mr. Davis cleared his throat and straightened his posture.

"You are late." Mr. Davis says.
I began to approach the stage.

"I know, I apologize. I just got bombarded with a bunch of things." I admitted.

"Hmph. Well, let's not waste anymore time. You are on the same team as you were last practice. Get prepared before I give you a topic."

I nodded my head as I placed my bag onto the floor. I sat down in my seat as I gathered different papers together. Once I was ready, I took a deep breath to clear my mind. As I turned my head, I saw Connor glance over at me. I rolled my eyes at him and gave my attention towards Mr. Davis. So much for having a clear mind. Just looking at Connor made my entire mind fog up with past memories. I can't stand the sight of him.

I pushed open the auditorium doors to be welcomed to the sight of Connor kissing the dirty blonde hair girl. The door shut behind me making my entrance louder than it needed to be. Connor removed his lips from hers as his face showed instant regret. The dirty blonde hair girl turned around and placed a hand on her hip.

"Look who it is." She announced as she drew closer to me. "Some of your bruises healed up quickly."

I clenched my jaw to prevent me from saying anything distasteful. The dirty blonde hair girl furrowed her eyebrows together as she drew even closer to me. Connor took notice of the altercation and began to pull her away from me.

"Come on, Hannah. Just leave her alone." Connor offered.

She wiggled out of his grasp and pointed her finger at me.

"Go ahead and start acting up because if you do, I'll be right there to knock you flat on your ass." She said as she sashayed away.

Connor stood there observing me. I can tell he wanted to say a lot of things but he was just frightened of my rebuttals. At this point in time, I can give less of a damn about what he would like to say to me. I am slowly getting over him and I really don't want any setbacks. I already have enough to deal with.

"Come on, Connor!" Hannah shouted from down the hall.

Before Connor made his way over to Hannah, he took a deep breath, adjusted his sleeve, and nodded at me. I watched him get chasisted by Hannah once he was walking alongside her. Now he knows how it feels to be dragged along like a rag doll.

"Jade."

I looked up to see Mr. Davis standing against the wall with his hands in his pockets. He motioned for me to enter inside of his office which I did. I took a seat in front of his desk as he stood by his chair.

"What's going on with you? You've missed four days of Debate practice and that's the most days you've missed since the three years you've joined this program." He started.

"Nothing. I've just been busy."
Mr. Davis gave me a look.

"Nothing? From the looks of that interaction you had with Hannah Farren it looks like something is going on. Is she the one that fought you in the cafeteria?"
I stayed quiet.

"She is, isn't she? Why didn't you tell the principal?" He asked.

"I thought I could handle it myself but once I realized I shouldn't stoop down to her level, I just let it go."

"That's noble of you. I understand your struggle in this school because I go through the same unfairness just like you do. All you have to do is lose your mind one time and they will know not to bother you again. Show them who the real Jade Morris is. The Jade Morris I know is someone who doesn't let anyone show her up and make a fool out of her."

I looked down and let out a sigh. Mr. Davis took notice and reached for something that was resting on the wall. He picked it up and held it in front of my face.

"In the long run it doesn't matter what I see. My question for you is what Jade Morris do you see?"

I looked into the mirror and observed myself. Two strips of my hair are plaited tightly against my scalp from front to back. The braids traveled to the upper portions of my breast where it rests comfortably. The baby hairs that rested on my hairline swooped into the start of my braids. Discoloration rested underneath my right eye as swelling took place on my eyelid. Tears soon welled into my eyes. As much as I tried to distract my hurt with my new hairstyle looking in the mirror made me realize that I am calling out for help. I was bringing more attention to myself to make people aware that I need assistance too. Being born with a darker pigmentation in the skin called melanin is wrongly set back as a disadvantage. I always felt the need to prove people wrong with what stereotype they had in their mind. Especially, when it comes down to me considering what neighborhood I live in and what influences I have. I just want to impact people's mindset and make a difference.

"I see..." I paused. "...a black girl trying not to be another statistic."

Mr. Davis placed the mirror back to its original position and looked at me with sympathetic eyes.

"Use that sense of character to win Finals tomorrow. Since you are the only black girl on this team, they will automatically doubt you and your abilities. Take that advantage and prove them wrong. You will get so much respect if you take that trophy from our rival school and place it on our trophy shelf with pride. Even if we don't win, I will still be in your corner rooting for you because you have so much potential to be something great. Understand?"

I nodded my head and took a deep breath. Mr. Davis landed his hand on my shoulder.

"Everything is going to be alright. You just have to keep your head up and keep striving for what you believe in. It'll all pay off in the end."

THIRTEEN

CONSTANT PRESSURE

A steady beat of rain bounced off of my closed window as the sound surrounded my entire room. Little droplets clung to the glass as the wind persuaded it to spread out amongst the surface. Rain made me more anxious. I found my mind being similar to the way my mom makes her eggs in the morning. Scrambled. I couldn't find anything to focus on. I was torn between decisions and it started to take a toll on my body. I keep getting recurring headaches along with low energy throughout the day.

I began to pace back and forth. I need to distract myself before I become trapped in my own thoughts. My stack of cards that help me prepare for Debate caught my eye as I let out a deep breath. I picked up the cards and began to look through them while taking a seat on my bed. As I was observing the cards, I heard Mr. Davis' encouraging words replay in my head. I stopped looking through the cards and began to breathe in stutters. I placed my attention up towards the ceiling and tried to calm down.

"Just get it over with." I whispered.

My phone rang as my stomach dropped. I placed the cards on my bed and stood up to attend to my phone.

"It's time." A familiar voice spoke to me.

Different cracks and gaps engraved the dampened sidewalk. My shoes squeaked as I carefully walked to try and keep myself from slipping. I landed my hands into my pockets to conserve as much body heat as I can. I stopped walking once I was welcomed to three men sitting on the stairs attempting to spark a cigarette. One guy looked up at me and narrowed his eyes. He soon pointed at me which gathered everyone's attention. Goosebumps arose on the back of my neck as I made a slight movement. I am in too deep right now. There is no turning back.

"You are that bitch that caused this house to get shot up." He announced as he stood up. "You must have a death wish for coming around here."

"I don't think I am the one that's wishing." I spoke as the two men that were sitting behind the guy shook their heads in disbelief. "I need to speak to Ricky."

"You got balls for a little girl, I'll give you that. He'll be glad to see you."

The man approached me and began to pat me down. In his failed attempt to find anything, he grabbed me by my collar and began to lead me inside of the house. The damages that were implemented in the house was soon getting repaired by Ricky's men. I let out a light chuckle and the guy took notice. He slightly pushed me towards the stairs as I held onto the railing to prevent me from falling. I gave him a look.

"Go ahead." He instructed with a smirk.

I began to walk down the stairs. Every creak from the steps filled me with anxiousness. I am just ready to get this ordeal over with. I really hope I can make it to Debate in time, it means so much to me. As I completed my descent, I saw Ricky bending over the pool table with his nose hovering above a clear plate. He soon straightened his posture, lifted his head up to the ceiling and let out a huge breath.

"Am I interrupting something?" I introduced as I folded my arms.

Ricky turned around and revealed himself to me. His eyelids were struggling to stay open as he placed his hand onto his forehead.

"Little trooper, how dare you bite the hand that fed you?"
I let out a sigh.

"Oh, please. You must really think I give a damn about you after all of the shit you have done. You're very delusional, Ricky."

He wiped his nose and began to approach me. Ricky's menacing eyes lurked all over my body as he made an approving sound.

"If you don't give a damn about me, explain to me why you're here to confess your sins." He started to laugh. "Jade, I like you. I can tell you mean business. Tell me why you are *really* here."

"I came here to seek answers."

"Answers? I'm sorry, sweetheart. I'm not a goddamn snitch. If you want answers, I suggest you take your little ass back out on the street and go searching for them. You've landed in the wrong spot and I don't take too kindly towards trespassers."

I stepped towards Ricky and looked up at him.

"Ricky, you can't do anything if your men are not protecting you or if your men are not getting their hands dirty for you. Your empty threats don't scare me."

"What are you talking about?"

Several loud thuds came from behind me as we both turned around in curiosity. A man laid on the floor with blood covering large spaces of his face. I had to close my eyes because if I took another look, everything I ate this afternoon would've been resting right next to him. I opened my eyes once I heard footsteps approaching. Andre and Regina finally made their descent with pistols in their hands. Ricky was about to dash towards his pool table to wield a gun but Andre let a chuckle which made Ricky stop in his tracks.

"I wouldn't do that if I were you. You know how I am with my gun, you really want to test your luck?" Andre spoke.

Ricky stopped and turned around to face us. He clenched his jaw and took a deep breath.

"I believe Jade came down here to respectfully ask for some answers. Now, if you don't do as she says, you'll end up like the rest of your buddies."

I felt out of my element. Regina and Andre are damn near professionals at this and I don't even know where to start. My mind began to race. I felt Regina's hand land onto my shoulder as she looked towards Ricky and nodded her head. I took a deep breath.

"My best friend, Michael Quinn was murdered by a middle class man. You assigned that individual to take him out. All I'm asking for is a name."
He began to laugh.

"You are doing all of this shit for him? If I had a ride or die like that—"

I kicked him in his leg as he got down on one knee. I grabbed at his throat and pulled him close.

"Does it look like I am playing with you? Give me a goddamn name."

"M-Michael had the same ambition as you and look where he is." He gasped as he placed his hand onto mine. "You are a dead woman walking if you think you can get anything out of me without anyone else hearing about it."

I looked towards Regina and held my other hand out. Regina furrowed her eyebrows together as I insisted for her to give me what I want. Her pistol grazed my fingertips as I wrapped my hand over it to get a tight grip. I placed the pistol onto his temple and clenched my jaw.

"This is the last time I am going to ask you. Give-me-a-name!"

Ricky hesitated and cursed underneath his breath. Our eyes connected as he let out a deep breath.

"Carl Koenig. That's the guy you're looking for."

I relaxed my hands as a smile parted my lips. Ricky held his neck and began to soothe it with his fingers.

"I have one more question for you." I started with a smirk. "Where do you find these middle class men?"

"Man, I don't know."

I gave him a doubtful look.

"You can get the rest of your answers from Koenig. I told you everything I know." He protested.

I let out a breath and nodded my head. I could tell he was hiding something but I didn't feel the need to pry. I got what I needed, it's no time to be greedy. Andre brushed past me and pinned Ricky against the wall. I furrowed my eyebrows in confusion as he looked over at us.

"I'll take care of him." He spoke as he faced his attention back on Ricky.

Regina tried to lead me upstairs but I refused.

"What is he about to do? He gave us what we wanted. Why are we continuing with—"

"It's best if we just go. Come on, Jade. Our work here is done." Regina explained.

We began our ascent up the stairs until I heard a gunshot. I stopped walking and held my head down while squeezing my eyes shut. I opened my eyes again and took a deep breath. Why is this victory so bittersweet? I feel like an animal. What I did back there was out of character and I don't know if I will ever be the same Jade Morris again. Wait, who really *is* Jade Morris? I saw her but I can't seek her soul through a reflected image.

FOURTEEN

FOCUS

The only audible essence you could hear was the tires constantly rolling over dips and uneven cement placements in the road. The uneasy silence that swelled in the car compressed against my ears as I constantly twiddled with my thumbs. My eyes were beginning to wander around in the front seats. I noticed that Andre sat comfortably behind the wheel as Regina absent-mindedly stared out of the window. It's like what happened a couple of moments ago completely escaped their minds. To the outside looking in, they appeared to be numb. They looked like robots, they expressed no type of emotion. Me on the other hand, I felt myself on the verge of tears. I'm constantly trying to put on a facade like nothing phases me but I tend to wear my emotions on my sleeve.

My mind began to explore my worries. I couldn't help but to be reminded of how late I am to the Debate competition. My anxiety began to tug at me which caused me to check my watch. Ten minutes late. I really hope they don't disqualify me or hell the entire team because of my tardiness. I let out a breath as I leaned forward in my seat.

"Are you sure you are going as fast as you can? I'm cutting it pretty close." I asked Andre.

He looked at me through the rear view mirror and placed his attention back on the road. I rolled my eyes and let out a breath. Regina turned around in her seat and forced a smile on her face.

"What he's really saying is *yes*. This car isn't exactly a Lamborghini."

"Oh, I noticed." I retorted as I looked up at the patch in the ceiling.

I took notice of Andre's frustration in the way he twitched his eyebrow in the mirror. A mere satisfaction welled inside me. A couple of minutes passed by until we finally rolled up in front of the school. I rushed out of the car and ran inside. Déjà vu hit me like a heavy truck as I was running through the hallways in my attempt to get to the auditorium. Once I reached my destination, I slowly opened the doors to not make the same mistake I made last time I was running late. I approached Mr. Davis and tapped him on his shoulder. A sense of relief filled him once he saw me. He gently pushed me towards the stage as I rushed up the stairs. My team cheered as they welcomed me to my seat. I noticed a smile part Connor's lips as he remained in his chair. My team began to take their rightful seats and settled down.

"Welcome, everyone to the tenth annual Debate competition!" The announcer presented.

Everyone that was spectating began to clap as my eyes wandered around in the crowd. "Let's begin with tonight's event! Our first topic is whether or not you think social networking sites are good for our society. Mount High, what's your argument?"

Connor stood up from his seat without consulting anyone which surprised all of us. I hope Connor knows that this competition is the *real* thing and not something he can just toy with. We are all supposed to work together as a collective and choose who shall go up there and represent our team. He soon took a deep breath before he prepared for what he had to say.

"Social networking is worshipped with false concepts of how people should act or be. Society is already in a confused swirl of accepting people who are different so why add the constant pressure of being the perfect guy or girl you see on social media? It's a very toxic environment that any child or teen can get caught up in." Connor spoke.

I noticed that sweat began to form on the side of his face.

"Jackson High, what's your counter argument?" The announcer asked.

A guy stood up and faced Connor. His dark brown eyes glared at him.

"Social media enabled many different opportunities for people to become successful at a young age. This highlights those particular people as role models amongst the youth which stimulates their motivation to accomplish their dreams. It also enables the opportunity for the world to become more connected."

"Hmph, you have a point. It does make the world more connected, *virtually*. But, it also enables a lot of social anxiety when you are just sitting on your phone all day *connecting* with people via text rather than going out and having real conversations. Think about it, social media is crippling. This society glorifies disrespect, sex and money. All of those things are sinful. You mean to tell me that those are examples for young children? I'm going to pray for your future kids."

"Time!" The announcer shouted as he approached the judges. "Who do you think took this round?"

I felt my stomach drop as I watched the judges pass their pieces of papers over to the judge on the end of the table. He calculated everything and made a final decision. He reached for the microphone as a smile parted his lips.

"Mount High!"

Our team began to celebrate as I swallowed hard. I leaned over the table and gathered everyone's attention.

"This is only the first round. It's still anybody's game. Make sure you are all ready for whatever topic is next." I coached as everyone began to nod their head.

"Alright, our second topic is whether or not you think refusing to stand for the National Anthem is an appropriate form of protest. Jackson High what's your statement?"

A Caucasian girl with dark brown hair stood up as she adjusted her pin on her jacket. She straightened her posture and made eye contact with the judges. The way she seemed so sure of herself intimidated the hell out of me. How can I - or anybody else - go up against someone like that?

"Refusing to stand up for the National Anthem is very disrespectful to the veterans that served and protected us from harm. Not having the dignity to stand and simply show respect for those who need it certainly defines their character. Those people feel as if their actions are justified - even when they are wrong - which results in very dangerous people. Lord knows we have enough of that." She stated as she pursed her lips.

The judges began to write things down on their notepads as they nodded their heads. The announcer faced our table which made my stomach drop.

"Mount High, what's your counter argument?"

Half of my team faced me and the other half faced Connor. Connor and I managed to make eye contact from the other side of the table. He lifted up his chin and lowered it back down. I took a deep breath before I stood up from my seat. I felt everyone's eyes plaster onto me. My body shook slightly as my breathing increased. I swallowed hard and tried to get my mind together.

"Mount High? You have a limited time to give your rebuttal. Speak now or give the round to them." The announcer warned.

I nodded my head and closed my eyes shut. I took several breaths before I opened my eyes and faced my opponent.

"Everyone has a choice in this world and sometimes that choice is shamed upon by others. A choice is usually decided on reasons and speculations that happened in their life or around it. Have you taken a step back and observed the restraints on a lot of communities? For example, the amount of blood on police officers' hands from an innocent man?" I felt my hand begin to shake. "Some Americans feel as if they are not as free as their country promises. Their average heroes are villains in their neighborhoods. Only way they would listen to the injustices is by making public statements. They kneel because their *veterans* were fighting against people who want to enslave and dictate our every move but they are not aware that the war that they are fighting outside has already stemmed inside their country."

The judges' faces expressed shock as some people in the crowd made a *hmph* sound.

"Really? That's your argument? You think America wants to *dictate* and *enslave* low income communities?" She asked me.

"They did it before. Don't try and polish up low income communities. We both know we are talking about minorities such as African Americans and other races that are not the perfect Caucasian image."

"This sounds racially biased. America had its ups and downs until it finally got back on its two feet and demanded order. Everything has been running as smooth as it can get. Everyone should sing the National Anthem because it symbolizes the growth of America and the strength we have to keep everyone safe."
I let out a light chuckle as the girl clenched her jaw.

"It's sad that people like you are so close minded. You don't have the empathy of those who are actually suffering in this community and who are victims of the system that will screw them over any chance it gets. Families of those imprisoned wrongly or their child's life taken away from them unjustly don't want to *respect* the Anthem. You give out what you are given. If they've been wronged, why should they worship a false ideation when they know America won't give two damns about them."

"Time!" The announcer spoke.

Everyone began to clap. I almost forgot I was in a room full of people. It felt as if it was just me and her in a room arguing. My team gave me a thumbs up as Connor laughed to himself.

"Judges, this is a very crucial part for this competition. If Mount High wins this argument, they can potentially win this entire competition and take home the trophy. So, who took this round?" The announcer asked as he got close to one of the judges.

The air thickened as the judge grabbed the microphone and held it towards his mouth. The process we all sat through before in the first round felt like years as they made up their final decision. Anticipation arose in my entire team as I felt my behind on the edge of the seat. This, is it.

"Mount High!"

My entire team stood up from their seats and began to hug me and shout my name. I felt as if my entire world turned from black to gray. A huge smile spread across my face as I sprung up from my seat. The announcer soon walked over to us and handed our team the trophy. One of my teammates came up to me and placed it into my hands. I looked at the trophy in awe as Mr. Davis' reflection appeared on the side. I looked up at him.

"I knew you could do it, kid." He said as he pulled me into a hug.

FIFTEEN

MELANIN ENTRY

Drug distribution has declined tremendously in various low income communities in Jackson, Mississippi. Although the certain change has brought many joys in the neighborhoods, there is still a high percentage in violence. It's been reported that fights have been more of an everyday thing considering there is nothing occupying the participants that chose to engage in these senseless scuffles. We need to stop fighting each other and start being more proactive in getting our lives back on track. If you have a criminal record and many jobs are declining you, I understand your frustration and your lack of motivation. You still have to keep searching for a profession to maintain stability. Don't allow the system to continue to break you. You are strong and capable of many things so don't allow them to belittle you. More cops have been roaming the neighborhoods in search of a petty case considering there are more people on the street. As much as you all want to rebel, just follow their directions and comply. If you do that, your *case* won't even make it to court. Please, stay safe out here. I don't want to report about anything else negative on this website. A change is going to come and I'm claiming it.

- Sincerely, Anonymous.

SIXTEEN

YEARN FOR CHANGE

Separate streams of water aligned onto my face as it saturated my exposed pores. It traveled from the tip of my round nose, towards my bold plump lips and onto my defined chest as it continued to explore various body parts. As the water began to crash down onto the floor, I soon felt the warmth exude off of the ceramic tile into the soles of my feet. The radiated heat engulfed my entire body as I gently held my head back in pure ecstasy. The water began to discover new places as it burst down onto my neck. After a few moments passed, I lifted my head back up to level out my blood flow. I soon reached for the faucet and turned it to the right. The water that was flowing so eloquently stopped abruptly as I stood in the middle of the tub soaking wet.

The places the water left its mark soon got replaced with dry skin from the soft towel. I wrapped it around my torso as I looked up at the fogged mirror. My hand slapped onto the surface as I drugged it vertically to reveal it's mocking presence. My eyes lurked around my reflection.

"What Jade Morris do you see?" Mr. Davis' voice repeated in my head.

My phone buzzed which took me out of my thoughts. I allowed the warm phone into my hands as I quickly read the message. I rolled my eyes once I realized the text was more of a demand that I have to fulfill.

"So much for a relaxing Sunday." I said underneath my breath as I locked my phone.

I landed my hand onto the glass door as I pushed forward to gain access inside the diner. Forks clicked off several plates as subtle conversations filled the entire room. The savoury smell of various foods hugged my nostrils as it traveled to the back of my throat leaving my mouth watering for food. I felt my stomach gnaw at itself to gather my attention towards the lack of nutrition in my system. I placed my hand onto my stomach as I rubbed in circles. I began to make my way over to a booth once my eyes landed onto a familiar face. Once I sat down and announced my presence, he didn't even bother to look up at me. His dark brown eyes were glued to his phone screen.

"I have something for you." He stated while he scrolled through his phone.

My right eyebrow twitched with curiosity.

"What is it?"

Andre placed his phone face down onto the table as he rummaged through his pockets. An envelope along with a flip phone was presented in front of me. I furrowed my eyebrows in confusion. He looked up at me, expectantly.

"What is all this?" I asked.

"See for yourself." He said as he leaned back in his seat.

I picked up the yellow envelope as I viewed the front side of it. There's no name nor an address listed on this envelope. My fingers edged towards the top as it slowly removed the flap from the body. My eyes lingered around the inside as I slowly figured out what was so discreetly hidden. I slowly backed up from the envelope as I looked up at Andre.

"Where did you get all of this money?" I whispered. A smirk creased his cheek.

"The answers you are seeking are in that phone."

I swallowed hard as my stomach dropped. I allowed the hinged phone into my grasp as I curiously observed its surface. I flipped the phone open as its screen lit up to greet me. I went through the contacts to see no numbers have been saved. There's also no information regarding the person who originally owned this phone. I clicked the messages to see a ton of unsaved numbers reaching out to this mysterious person. Most of the messages are just demands for the other person to accomplish. I'm also seeking a pattern here. The person that wielded this phone is the main person giving out the demands. The demand details are drug distributions. I placed my elbows onto the table as I continued with my search.

"Is there anything I can get you two?" I heard a voice ask.

I removed the phone from my face as I looked up at the server. My mom made a face once she recognized me.

"Coffee would be fine." Andre ordered.

My mom wrote down his order and then glared at me.

"The usual?" She asked as her lip turned up.

I lifted my eyebrow in response to her comment. She rolled her eyes and walked away from our table. Andre took notice of our interaction and clenched his jaw.

"That's your mom?"

"That obvious, huh?" I asked through a breath.

"You aren't close with her?"

I sighed.

"Not at all. She's just my roommate and coworker." I responded.

"That's unfortunate." He commented, coldly.

"Well, that's life, Andre. You're not the only person that has that."

His eyebrows furrowed with frustration.

"Just..." He paused. "...finish looking through that phone."

I rolled my eyes as I pressed the home button to wake up the phone. Once the screen allowed me to journey through again, I took advantage of that opportunity. I happen to stumble upon a familiar number. My heart dropped as I clicked on the message. My eyes frantically traveled around the words as my mind couldn't properly digest the information I was receiving.

"M-Michael." I trembled underneath my breath.

A lump formed in my throat as I tried to keep my composure. This is Ricky's phone. Michael was trying to negotiate a way for Ricky to lower the price so he can get him off of his back but Ricky wouldn't let up. I covered my mouth with my right hand as I gripped the phone with my left. This must be the phone that Ricky used to contact the officer. I looked through the remaining messages from chronological order to try and pinpoint the actual set up. After the constant scrolling, I finally found it. Ricky paid Koenig to take out Michael. Ricky felt as if he was a threat to his operation and he needed someone with higher skill to take him out as quickly as they could. Ricky didn't want one of his guys doing this job because he knew Michael was smarter than him. He knew that he would've easily gotten away just like how his brother slipped out of his hands the first time Ricky sent his men out on him.

I stared at Koenig's phone number with pure hatred in my eyes. My entire mindset shifted. I was drawn to the idea of restoring justice for Michael. If that means, hurting Koenig, then so be it.

"Why did you show me this?" I asked with tears in my eyes.

"You're good with computers. That number you found, it's our shot to finding the officer that murdered Michael. Once we find him, we can get more answers to finish setting our neighborhood back to the way it used to be. Just imagine the peace and tranquility, Jade."

My mind began to explore the possibilities Andre was proposing to me. Peace is the most desired thing our neighborhood has yearned for, for years. My neighborhood now has changed. I no longer hear the comforting sound of children laughing whenever

I walk through the streets of my neighborhood. In replacement of the laughter, I hear distant shouting in various buildings. You can feel the tension rise upon your neck as it sends shivers down your spine. That alone, forced everyone to be on edge. I just want our community back. I looked up at Andre.

"When we find him, I'm going to take care of him, personally."

SEVENTEEN

_____

RAW EMOTION

Hazel gripped onto her iris as it tried to stay on considering how fast she was moving her eyes across the phone's screen. Her eyebrows drew closer to her eyelids as her brain was quickly gathering the information she was receiving. Creases slowly appeared onto her forehead due her facial muscles contracting so abruptly. Her lips were tucked underneath her top row of teeth as she clenched them together. Regina's face wreaked of pure emotion. The feeling she felt the day of the funeral was ignited back like a wildfire. She attempted to bottle it up and not allow any *oxygen* in to continue the spread but even I know how difficult that is. I give her credit for keeping it in as long as she did.

Regina's eyes dampened as I moved over to comfort her. I wrapped my arms around her as I squeezed her back tightly. She was in too much shock to complete the hug I offered to her. I didn't mind it, though. I know what she's going through. I looked up at Andre to see him staring at us through sympathetic eyes. I met his stare, expectantly. Andre rubbed his chin as he began to look away. I rolled my eyes as I began to pull away from Regina. I placed my hands onto her face to wipe away her tears.

"This Koenig is a coward. Taking a young man's life over money he wasn't responsible for is not what I'm going to tolerate." I began as I removed my hands from her face. "I'm going to get justice for him. By any means necessary."

"Jade, you can't confront him." Regina sniffled. "You out of the three of us can't take him down. You saw how he tossed around Michael. You really think you can be any different?"

"Yes. I've allowed these emotions to harvest and fester throughout my body for an entire year. You don't know what I am capable of."

Andre turned his head to look at me and furrowed his eyebrows together. He slowly approached me as I stood up from the couch, defensively.

"You're unstable, Jade. One wrong move with him can cost you your entire life. Now, stop your bullshitting. We have work to do." Andre spat.

"You don't know anything about me." I retorted.

"Come on, guys." Regina interjected through a breath.

"I know for a fact you'll crack under pressure." I clenched my jaw while stepping closer to him.

"I won't. I know that for a *fact*." I tested. Andre licked his lips as he looked at Regina.

"They have to learn someday." He said.

In a quick movement, Andre's hand wrapped around my neck. His large fingers dug into the sides of my throat. The palm of his hand forced my neck to bend backwards which directed my head to be thrown back. In the corner of my eye, I could see Regina shaking her head in disbelief. Why isn't she helping me? The airway obstruction caused panic throughout my body once I realized how quickly air was escaping from my lungs. I frantically dug my nails into his arm to try and stop him.

"How do you expect to take down Koenig when you can't even get the upper hand on me?" He asked as his grip tightened.

My head felt light as my eyes became heavy.

"I-I can." I gasped.

"Alright, that's enough." Regina said.

Andre looked at her and then back at me. Something in his eyes changed once he realized how much he was in the wrong. He released his hand from my neck as I crashed down onto the floor. Air slowly took its rightful place into my lungs as I heard feet shuffling towards the front door. Through my blurred eyes, I saw Andre leave the apartment while Regina stood in the corner of the room. She folded her arms as she looked down at me.

"Why didn't you help me!" I yelled as I held my throat.

"I'm not always going to be there to save you, Jade. Why'd you have to provoke him?"

"I didn't! I was just standing up for myself. I'm so tired of being pushed around by people that think I can't do anything for myself. I'm sick of it! I don't..."

I paused. "...I don't need you guys. You guys need me way more than I need you all. Just get out of my house."

"Jade—"

"Get out!" I shouted once more.

Her face twisted with sadness as she turned her back to me. I felt my eyes well up with tears until I immediately wiped them away with my forearm. She finally completed her exit. The door's closing echoed around the room as I staggered up to my feet. I made my way towards the bathroom until I crashed into the wall. I landed my hand onto the surface as I caught my breath. Once I gathered myself, I made my way into the bathroom. I turned on the light and glared at the mirror. The bruises wrapped around my neck like a snake about to attack its prey. I placed my fingers onto my neck and slowly traced the bruises' trail. My eyes lurked around my wound until anger arose in my chest. I placed my hands onto the edge of the sink and got close to the mirror. My breathing increased. Before I knew it, I slammed my fist into the mirror causing it to split down the middle. The mirror reflected a distorted image of myself as I tilted my head to the right. Blood ran down the mirror as a smile parted my lips.

"I see you, Jade. Now, he's going to see me."

EIGHTEEN

BIRTH OF A MADWOMAN

This may be my last post on this website. I'm sorry to all of those people that look forward to my posts and daily uplifting but I can't live with myself knowing I am just a big hypocrite. I've succumbed to my anger and sorrow and it has turned me into a person I've never thought I'd become. I don't want to feed you all with advice knowing the source you're getting it from is just a dying rose that had acid poured all over it. You all deserve better and will get better once I get down to the bottom of all of this chaos. If I become a martyr in the process just remember me as a person that just wanted better for our society. People of color, please start encouraging one another and embracing others with your love. Love goes a long way. Trust me, I know. I've been stripped of love at a young age and I've been broken ever since. Until this young man with a goofy smile came into my life. He mended those broken parts within me with his love and support. I never knew life could be so worth living until one day an officer murdered him in cold blood. You've guessed it, a police officer murdering another bright young man but not in the *regular* sense. For the sake of my identity, I will keep his name disclosed and handle him personally. On the other hand, I have configured a pattern. Dirty cops are murdering people who have a debt on their hands. The debt entails how much money they owe from the drugs they sell but get this. People who go out and sell those drugs are people who have no other choice. Given our living conditions, we all need money. Some more than others. These people are sold on a dream and yet get settled with a nightmare. They're given a short amount of time to sell a huge portion of their product just to please the boss of the operation. Drug dealers are lower class men, dirty cops are middle class men and the person that orchestrates this entire operation is the upper class man. I'm going to restore peace amongst our neighborhoods. Stay safe and stay woke. This has been your hood hero.

- Sincerely, Anonymous.

NINETEEN

FAITH OVER FEAR

My head laid back in the car seat as I watched his house sit perfectly still. I looked down at the middle compartment to see my pistol laying there attentively. My eyebrow lifted once my eyes shifted onto the rear view mirror. I didn't want to conceal my face. I want him to see the pain behind my eyes and the stress that lives underneath my skin. I want this to be intimate. If I can't get him to understand my hurt I could at least make him acknowledge it. I pulled out my phone and hit the camera option. I hit record and immediately placed it back into my pocket. A subtle breeze squeezed through the cracked open window. The wind caressed the back of my neck as it sent shivers down my spine. I took a deep breath. This is the day justice is served for Michael's murder.

I stood there as a piercing sensation struck my lower abdomen. Loud ringing filled my ears as I stumbled backwards. My eyes were fixated on Koenig as he rushed over to his wife. My anxiety spiked once I realized his wife was Ms. Collins. I couldn't wrap my head around this piece of information. It seemed unbelievable. Out of all people to be married to this bastard, it just had to be her. I looked down at my stomach to see blood seeping through my shirt. I cautiously landed my hand onto my wound which made my head feel lighter than what it was. My back pressed up against the wall as I slowly lowered down to the floor. I began to claw at my wound considering it started to burn the surrounding area. It felt like the gates of hell threw a party in my stomach. I let out a cry as I pressed my head up against the wall.

Once the pain eased, I looked over to see Koenig hovering above Ms. Collins. Blood was everywhere. Fear pulled onto my heartstrings as I tried to remain calm. I want to keep my vulnerability at a minimum considering I can still oppose a threat regardless of my injuries.

"Katelyn!" He yelled as he placed his two hands onto her wound. "Stay with me, dammit."

Ms. Collins managed to move her head over to glance at me. Her eyes widened with shock once she recognized me. I furrowed my eyebrows together because I couldn't bare to see her like this. Hardened skin gripped her lips as it began to spread amongst the surface. In the dips of the lips' skin, blood rested attentively as a few droplets rolled down the side of her cheek. Her face was drained of her natural color, leaving her of a pale complexion. Her pupils dilated with fear as she slowly observed me.

"J-Jade." She whispered.

My heart dropped.

"Who the hell is that?" Koenig questioned as he followed her stare.

His dark brown eyes made its way over to me as it gleamed with hatred. He slowly rose up to his feet as he drew closer to his gun that was resting on the floor next to Ms. Collins. She managed to grab his arm before the gun made it into his grasp.

"Don't." She said as she squeezed his wrist. "What happened?"

His thinning eyebrows drew closer together to create a crease in between. His temples tightened as his breathing slowly increased. His body language shouted frustration but you can feel the radiating hesitation wreaking from his pores.

"How do you know her name?" He asked, sternly.

Ms. Collins gave a weak smile.

"Student. I'm going to ask you one more time, what happened?"

Pain ripped through me as I gritted my teeth together. I landed my hand onto my wound and pressed it down. I took a deep breath.

"He murdered a seventeen year old boy on duty." I interjected.

They both looked over at me.

"What are you talking about? What kid?" He shouted.

I noticed sweat started to travel down the side of his temple as his eyebrows departed from one another.

"Y-You know exactly who I am talking about." I retorted.

Ms. Collins shook her head in disbelief as Koenig clenched his jaw.

"Is it true?" She asked through a cough.

"You're going to believe this hoodlum over me?" He asked through narrowed eyes. Ms. Collins shot him a look. Koenig's face flushed with emotion as he tried to maintain his composure. "You do, don't you."

Ms. Collins looked away and closed her eyes. A tear rolled down the side of her cheek as she clenched her jaw. Koenig faced me which sent shivers down my spine. He managed to wiggle out of Ms. Collins' grasp and grabbed his pistol. Ms. Collins shouted Koenig's name as he slowly drew closer to me.

"My job was to pull the trigger, don't hold me accountable for taking his life."

"That mentality is the reason why you are going to rot in hell." I looked down at his pistol and back up at him. I pushed everything I had into my feet as I slowly rose up. Tears stained my cheeks as we connected eyes over the barrel of his drawn gun. "Do what you have to do. You already took the only thing that made me happy and ran over it like roadkill in the street! People like you make me sick and I don't want to become like you."

I looked down at the floor and swallowed hard. Once I gathered myself, I re-established eye contact with him.

"I forgive you. I've been holding onto this pain for too long and look where it's gotten me. I don't know what motivated you to become the person you are but I hope God has mercy on your soul."

Koenig clenched his jaw as he looked away from me. Apologizing to someone who shows that they're not even sorry just displays how strong of a person I am. For that, I was rewarded with the sensation of a breath of new life. It felt like I could fully breathe. This new revelation filled my heart with pure joy as I soon became at ease with everything in my life. I looked down at Ms. Collins with sympathetic eyes.

"Thank you for trying to help me. I guess you were right—"

I collapsed to the floor. The impact between my face and the floor made my head feel like broken antiques that got damaged by a bull in a China shop. I heard my name being called in the distance but before I could respond my body completely shut down. When you're close to death you might think it is frightening but it is the most peaceful thing you could ever experience. Should I stay in that peace or keep thriving in this cold world?

EPILOGUE

In the shadow of death, I feared no evil. The warmth of His comfort shielded me from the blistering cold as I embarked on a divine serenity. I've sought my life as a table He prepared for me in the presence of my enemies. Staring at them in the eyes makes me realize that there is not much of a difference between them and me. Pride, envy, gluttony, lust, anger, greed and sloth seeped through their bloodstreams and rewired their hearts to become an evildoer. It programmed me to do the same until I held my hands up and resisted at the very last second. Time suddenly came to a halt as I realized I was enclosed into a small box. It's limit of space became very frightening which sent me into a panic. Mentally and physically. I knew I needed to be released. With a lot of strength and courage, I broke free of the glass and ventured onto a new path. If I would've continued my sturt to utter chaos, I would've killed a man or ended up dead. Why did God decide to spare me?

As I lay on top of a stretcher, my eyes become fixated on the subtle pastel colors that advanced across the sky. A breeze caressed the side of my face as I closed my eyes. My cheeks became cold as tears saturated my pores. A smile parts my lips as I open my eyes to watch God paint the sky. I should've listened to Him a long time ago. God isn't going to shout in your face to gather your attention. You have to be willingly open to His advice and silent enough to hear His silentious whispers. He would've told me a long time ago to stop living the same year over eighty times and labeling that as my life. Instead, I should've sat at the table He anticipated and concluded events in my life the right way to earn my anointment. I've come to realize that as well as His reason for sparing me. I've been through hell and back and I am still on this Earth with a smile on my face. It's about time I start doing things in God's way and brightening up places that have been dark a long time.

Jade will return...

Made in the USA
Monee, IL
20 January 2022

89378385R10073